The Spider

A Muldoon Mystery: Book One
Hanna Delaney

To my husband and my girls,
for whom my love knows no bounds.

Part I

1

Stepping out of the carriage to look at number five, Percy Street, Frances Bryant gasped. Her new home stood at an impressive four stories, with an ornate gabled roof and striking red brickwork. The beauty of it brought a lump to her throat. "This is our house?" she asked her husband, who was watching the nanny lift their daughter out of the carriage. The coach driver inspected the interior for any forgotten belongings and, satisfied that there was nothing there, gently closed the door, bowing to the little girl with a kind smile.

From the outside, the house was what her mother would have described as 'grand'. A grand house, with a green lawn, glistening white paint on the window frames and floors upon floors of space. It stood neatly contained among a row of complementary siblings, all proudly facing the street. Their gardens displayed their prosperity; their bricks displayed their wealth.

John Bryant stood beside his wife on the pavement, placing an arm around her waist. Frances felt that at any moment, she would wake up and be back in the cottage she had shared with her mother. "It's ours," John said, pointing the handle of his umbrella to the tall, black varnished door that stood within a pillared porch. "You can thank Australia." She looked up at his handsome, chiselled face. His grey eyes pierced through his tan like diamonds in the dirt. She felt a buzz of electricity power through her body as his lips landed on her cheek. She felt his moustache brush against her soft skin; although his new fashion statement tickled her, it added to his charming character, she thought. At that moment, they could have been the only people on the street, for she couldn't take her eyes off him. Only one day before, it had been four years since she had last seen John Bryant.

"It feels like a dream."

Birds chirped in the dense trees overhead as the driver lifted their belongings out of the back of the cab. John ensured that the old man was paid and thanked. The horses, under firm instruction, trotted into action, taking the cab back the way they had come, leaving the Bryant family and their nanny on the doorstep of number five. "Shall we?" John asked, raising an eyebrow.

"John, you're making me nervous," she said, taking to the steps with a giggle. He removed his hat and unlocked the door. Frances, on closer inspection, could see that it was freshly painted. "Don't touch it darling," she said to her little girl.

Elspeth 'Elsie' Bryant was four years old. She stood in a green velvet dress trimmed with black ribbon and held the hand of her nanny, Sarah Jones. Sarah, a young woman in her early twenties, had been an agreeable choice for a nanny when Elsie was a baby.

More importantly, Elsie adored her. The family had been living in a small cottage in West Derby until John returned from Australia with what he called "a small fortune," and swiftly moved them to the eastern part of the city.

John stepped in first, hanging his hat on the stand. The black and white tiles that decorated the hall were brand new. "They finished just yesterday," John remarked as the women admired the craftsmanship. He hooked his umbrella on the coat stand and, with the familiarity of a man who had lived there for years, checked himself in the hall mirror.

"John, this house is beautiful," Frances said, looking up at the white, high ceilings with their decorative cornices and festoons. The chandelier in the hall seemed enormous. She wanted to cry.

To Frances' surprise, waiting for them at the foot of the stairs were two women. The mid-morning sun had met the window of the landing, passing white beams down the stairs that silhouetted the two figures at first. As her eyes adjusted to the light, Frances could see them in more detail. One was a young, thin maid with a pasty, freckled face and long, bony limbs. The other, an older lady. Both wore white lace caps and aprons. "Frances, this is our maid, Maggie," John said, introducing the first one.

"Good morning, ma'am," Maggie said with a curtsey, revealing some rebellious strawberry blonde curls that tried to burst out on her return to standing upright. John raised an arm toward the older lady, "and this is Mrs Mckinnon, our housekeeper."

"Housekeeper?" Frances asked, taken aback by the announcement.

"Unless you want to run all of this by yourself, of course?" John opened his arms and twirled around the hallway. Frances shook her head. She did not want to manage four stories by herself.

"That's wonderful," she said. "Pleased to meet you. I'm Frances," she said, reaching out a hand. Mrs Mckinnon took it enthusiastically.

"It's lovely to meet you Mrs Bryant, ma'am."

"Mrs Mckinnon and Maggie are with us every day except Sunday when they finish at twelve," John added. "The gardener comes every fortnight on a Monday."

"Wonderful," was all Frances could think to say. Mrs Mckinnon, almost sensing the impending silence, bent down to look at Elsie.

"And you must be Elspeth!" Mrs Mckinnon remarked, smiling at the little blonde girl hiding behind the nanny's skirts.

"Elsie can be quite shy, Mrs Mckinnon," said Sarah apologetically.

"Ach, I'm a strange old woman today. She'll get used to me, I'm sure." Mrs Mckinnon rummaged in her pocket and produced a small, boiled sweet. Elsie silently approached her and took the sweet like a little bird, retreating back to her hiding spot behind Sarah. Mrs Mckinnon laughed.

Frances took a moment to study the new housekeeper. Violet Mckinnon was a ruddy-faced Scotswoman in her fifties. She

wore a tight silver bun at the nape of her neck and had a beautiful smile. She was a short, stout woman and had small, crescent
glasses resting at the edge of her nose. "I wonder if anybody
here likes scones? I make scones and cakes and buns, but only if
everyone eats them."

"I'm sure that won't be a problem you're faced with," said
Frances, looking back at Elsie who had reappeared from behind
Sarah. Mrs Mckinnon laughed again. "Let us take the bags,
ma'am."

Without a word, Maggie stepped forward to collect a bag and
took it upstairs. She was gangly and thin, but clearly she had
hidden strength. Frances, aware of her own clumsy tendencies,
stepped back, allowing them to gather the luggage without any
obstacles and watched them disappear as they ascended the
staircase.

"John," Frances whispered, "servants?"

He seemed surprised by her question. "Of course. I told you
I wouldn't come back unless I could give you a better life. You
and Elsie, that is."

"We can afford servants?"

"We can afford servants. They live downstairs in the basement, but there's a bell in every room should you need them
outside of their duties."

Frances stared at him for a moment. He stood before her
pristinely dressed, with his moustache waxed , a new pocket
watch and polished shoes. She looked down at her own clothes
and cringed. She wore a grey wool travelling dress and old but

well-loved boots. Her daughter, she noticed, was dressed better than she was. She felt out of place in the grand house as she caught herself in the mirror. Her face, although she felt it was amiable, looked tired.

Behind John stood a grandfather clock. Its hands were fixed on five minutes past twelve. "That's not the time, is it?" Frances asked. John retrieved his pocket watch from his jacket and checked.

"No, it needs winding," he said, removing his jacket and hanging it on the stand. He set to work on it immediately. "Well, don't wait for me. Go and explore," he said, noticing her still standing there watching him. Sarah, without a moment's pause, had followed Elsie out into the garden. Frances hung around for a moment longer before deciding on the parlour room.

As she had expected, it was a grand room with elegant furniture and a decorative fireplace that made her look twice. She found herself in the centre of the room, staring at it. The mirror above it bounced the light from the window into her eyes, blinding her. Rushing over to close the drapes, she clumsily crashed into a small ornament on the window ledge. "Oh no," she whispered as she quickly caught it. It was a little figurine of a boy playing a flute. She inspected it quietly and sighed when she saw that he was still intact. Like a child wishing to hide their accidents from their mother, she looked over her shoulder and quietly, quickly restored him to his resting place. To her surprise, her hands were shaking.

She shuffled out of the room and back into the hallway. The ticking of the grandfather clock could be heard now. John closed the casing and took a cigar from the box on the sideboard of the hall, lighting it with a match from his pocket.

"Just needed winding," he said, admiring it. "Where have you been?"

"The parlour room. It's beautiful."

"I hoped you'd like it."

"I do!" she exclaimed. "It's almost as big as the entire cottage."

"You'll become accustomed, I'm sure," he said, inhaling some of the cigar and blowing it up into the air. "There's something you might like in the drawing room. Close your eyes."

With his cigar fixed firmly between his lips, he took her hands in his and gently guided her to the middle of the drawing room where she stood still, waiting. She could feel her heart thumping in her chest, not knowing what she was about to see.

"You can open them now."

The drawing room was large and well lit, with glass-panelled doors and a small garden outside. Frances spotted the cottage piano in the corner and clasped her hands over her mouth. John laughed at her reaction and lowered his cigar. "Well?" he asked.

"I haven't... I haven't played in years."

Since before they were married, she realised. It looked identical to the piano that her parents had when she was growing up; it was so old that she couldn't be sure that it *wasn't* the piano she had had growing up. Frances approached it excitedly and brushed a hand across the polished wood, smiling to herself as she did so. It seemed strangely familiar, compelling her to touch it.

"Are you going to play now?" John asked, leaning on the mantelpiece. She sat down on the stool with a thump, having misjudged the distance and after laughing at herself, lifted the lid carefully, tapping a couple of keys.

Eventually, a melody came to mind and she let her fingers explore the notes. She smiled to herself as she played.

2

FRANCES HADN'T NOTICED JOHN'S disappearance as she played her repertoire. *I don't blame him*, she thought. *I'm rather unpractised.* Wanting to see the rest of the house, she closed the lid over the keys and admired her piano one more time. She thought it was beautiful, but she wanted to see more of her new home and find where John had gone. With her skirts rustling in the silence of the enormous house, she ascended the stairs in search of him.

The master bedroom waited for her at the top of the first set of stairs. Inside it hung another chandelier above a four-poster bed. Her heart stopped when she came inside the room and saw the fresh rose petals on the linen. On the dresser was a decorative wooden box. She opened it gingerly. Inside were six chocolates. She took one and nibbled it.

She had not realised that John was waiting behind the door of the bedroom. "I hoped you'd find those," he said, closing it behind him. She gasped, and frightened by the sudden surprise, started choking on the chocolate she had just accidentally inhaled. She had not even sensed his presence, or smelled the cigar smoke. "I'm sorry," he said, laughing. "I didn't mean to scare you." The coughing finally ceased and they both laughed.

"Do you mean to kill me, John Bryant?"

"Absolutely not," he purred. "I didn't buy this house so I could be a widower in it." He took another pull from his cigar and released the clouds of smoke into the bedroom. Frances, having never been a fan of tobacco, went over to the other end of the room and opened the sash slightly. The hustle and bustle of the city outside quietly penetrated the silence of their bedroom. Sweet summer air blew in, replacing the slight staleness with a welcome freshness. She could see the river in the distance, twinkling in the peach haze of the afternoon sun as steamships sailed across the water. Out there, grey clouds of smoke from the factories rose into the sky as though from the nostrils of a sleeping dragon. In their house on the hill, she felt like a princess, gazing down at her kingdom from the comfort of her chambers. Miles of rooftops and greenery unfolded before her, rolling into the horizon like a watercolour painting.

"It's really something, John. I can't quite believe it." She looked out at the cobbled street and thought the rows of trees were so neat, like green beacons of hope standing up against the soot-covered buildings that she had been used to seeing on the waterfront. The comforting clip clop of hooves passing by reminded her that she was really there, really at home.

"It's all ours. There is one condition though."

Frances turned to look at him. His usual playful, carefree expression was partly obscured by heavy, downcast brows. She held her breath. He looked at her concerned face and smiled. "You must come to dinner with me whenever I ask."

Her shoulders relaxed and she shook her head. "Oh, desist with the games, John!" She walked over to the tall, oak wardrobe and inspected its contents. Various silks, furs and gowns hung from the rail, taking her aback. She didn't recognise any of them as hers. "John... are these—?"

"Yours? Of course they are. If we're going out to dinner, you'll need new dresses." He watched her pull out a red evening gown trimmed with lace and velvet. "I thought you'd like that one most of all." She held it to her chest and looked at herself in the tall mirror of the wardrobe. She thought that it was beautiful; she thought that *she* was beautiful.

"I do like it."

"Well, you can wear that one this week when I take you for dinner," he said, leaving the room. "Thursday night at the Adelphi."

Frances smiled and placed the gown back into the wardrobe delicately. As she pushed the skirt back in, she noticed that it smelled different, with a whiff of a fragrance that she didn't recognise at first: Lavender. Realising that it had been so long since she had had new clothes, she wondered if the latest fashion was to have them made already perfumed. She looked down at her old, dull, woollen travelling gown and shrugged the notion off.

When she reached for the brass knob on the door of the bedroom, she was slowed by the sound of something creaking behind her. She sharply turned around to find that the door of the wardrobe was open, with the red skirt having unfolded and pushed its way out. She hurried back over to it and stuffed it in some more, closing the door firmly. She heard the magnet inside click and, satisfied with the second attempt at closure, left the room.

In the next room along the landing, there was a guest bed and some furniture similar to that of her bedroom. She walked in and went straight to the window. Elsie and Sarah were in the garden; Sarah had already drawn a hopscotch grid with chalk and was hopping across the squares, much to Elsie's delight. Frances backed away from the window and sat down on the bed for a moment. The guest bedroom was another grand room, fragranced with various bowls and vases of dried flowers and herbs. Warm from the closed window and strong sunshine, Frances lay down on the bed and dozed.

She didn't know how long she had been sleeping for when she was awoken by the deafening whistle of the kettle.

Downstairs, Mrs Mckinnon had served tea in the parlour room. Frances thanked her graciously and rushed to sit down and pour herself a cup. John sat on the sofa opposite, reading a paper. She leaned back and admired him over the rim of her cup.

"See something you like?" he asked, not looking up. She laughed at having been caught.

"Yours is a face I have not seen for a long time, John Bryant. I was trying to etch it into my consciousness," she said quietly. He grinned and put the paper down on the coffee table.

"I'm not going anywhere, you know. At least not until winter."

"By then it shall be too soon."

"Are you happy here?"

"Incredibly so."

"Did you enjoy your sleep?"

"I didn't know I needed it."

"It pleases me to see how relaxed you feel here. I was worried you'd hate it."

"Why?"

"You were so used to the cottage. You were so used to your mother."

"She'll be all right. I've invited her here on Wednesday."

"Oh?"

"Don't look at me like that, John. She ought to see the house, don't you think?"

"I suppose. I wonder if I have an appointment on that day... all day perhaps," he said, rubbing his chin.

"John!"

"I'm teasing. I hope she likes it. Perhaps I'll go up in her estimations, who knows?"

Frances smiled and shook her head. "She must be impressed. It's not every day your daughter's husband returns from the other side of the world and surprises her with a house and servants."

"Good. It's all for you, you know." He sipped his tea and looked around the room. "I wanted it to be like new, as though I was bringing my new bride to her first house."

"We can pretend that that is exactly what this is."

"If you say so." He winked and reached for his paper again. "You like it then?"

"I think it's splendid," she said, fixing her gaze on the ornate mantelpiece once more. She was happier than she could find the words to express; not wanting to ruin the peace of the moment, she suppressed any further questions about Australia or his long absence and, knowing she had little will left to avoid talking about it, filled her twitching mouth with tea instead of words.

The clock in the hallway began to chime, which surprised Frances as she glanced at the mantel clock that said it was half past two in the afternoon. The chimes continued. She listened, counting them.

"That blasted clock," John said, slamming the paper down on the table. "It's stuck on twelve again."

"Perhaps we need it mended," she said.

"Perhaps we need it hammered to pieces," he said, rolling his sleeves up. With a look of disdain, he marched out of the room.

3

Frances, having not yet explored the nursery, ventured upstairs. When she reached the top of the second staircase, she found that there was a long landing with only one door at the end. The long wall was adorned with various paintings of people and places. Much smaller copies of famous works by Monet and more recent impressionists whose names she couldn't remember stood proudly, overlooking the highest floor of the house in gilded frames.

"Elsie?" she asked, "are you there?" She slowly approached the panelled door and listened first. Frances reached for the knob and turned it clockwise. The door opened with ease as she peered in to see an empty nursery.

Frances looked across the room to the open window, still unable to accept that this was her view now. Across the street, there were passers-by walking on the pavement and conversing outside the church. Horses trotted past carrying various loads, nodding as they pulled their carriages, trams and carts to their destinations. Everything was as expected, but a part of her felt that it would all fall away and reveal itself to have been merely a trick: something that could have been, not something that *was*.

Burying the doubt once more, she turned around to look at the nursery again. It looked as though Sarah and Elsie had already explored their new rooms, placing their things on the beds and changing out of their travel clothes. Frances picked up Elsie's little green dress from the bed and hung it in the wardrobe that stood against the partition wall to Sarah's bed. Frances, on closer inspection, thought that the side room where Sarah slept was cleverly designed; Elsie could have her own room with her nanny always within arm's reach.

Unlike other parts of the house, it was not the fumes of fresh paint that reached her nostrils in this room, it was a floral fragrance. As with her bedroom on the first floor, there were bundles of potpourri stationed on every surface, resting in little dishes on dressers and above the wardrobe. They smelled of rosemary and lavender. She thought of the red dress and suspected that there was potpourri in her wardrobe, too.

The teddy bears and rocking horse reminded her of her own nursery when she was small. She pushed the horse gently and watched it glide back and forth on its runners. Its expression, although carved and permanently set, seemed cheerful.

She loved the nursery. It had plenty of room for play. As she admired the teddy bears of various shapes, colours and sizes, Frances wondered if they would have any more children to fill the enormous room with. Elsie had been their only child due to John's work arrangements. The thought of being alone for several years more made her shudder. She wondered if that was over now as she examined the toys and the furniture in the room. There were so many toys. Too many for one girl.

The little bed where her daughter would sleep had a curtained canopy. Elsie had called it a "princess bed." Frances sat down on it and admired the decor and linens of the room. John really had thought of everything. Rows of pretty dolls sat against a wall, each decorated with their own frilly frocks, bows and bells. Frances admired them all, wondering how much John had had to pay for them. He hadn't discussed specific numbers but, judging from the clothing she had seen and the house he had just moved them to, she felt that it must have been enough to buy all of these toys as well. She picked one of the little dolls up and held it. It had tight black curls and blue glass eyes that stared back at her.

"That's Blissy," said a little voice behind her. Frances felt her heart leap and kick back into action again as she looked down at her daughter.

"Goodness, you scared Mummy, sweetheart."

"Blissy is new. She has lots of sisters," Elsie said calmly. She was wearing a lighter, blue frock with a broderie anglaise skirt. It was incredibly similar to the frilly dress that Blissy was wearing. Frances looked back at her daughter and then at the dolls sitting against the wall.

"Oh she certainly does, doesn't she? How are they all feeling about the new house?"

"It's not new for them," Elsie said. "They've been here for a long time."

Their strange conversation was abruptly executed when the little bell on the wall of the nursery rang. Frances, not knowing what it meant, slowly approached the landing, held her breath and listened. Downstairs, she could hear the kettle whistling again.

Frances sat at the kitchen table with Elsie while Sarah prepared supper for her, making some tea for Frances in the process. Frances thanked her and took the cup gratefully, sipping on the steaming liquid. Despite the summer evening sunshine outside, she felt the need to warm herself.

"Ach, you should have let me do that, Sarah," said Mrs Mckinnon, entering the room with a basket of fruit and vegetables in her arms. She laid it down on the kitchen table. Elsie's eyes lit up at the sight of cherries, which rested with their shiny red skins atop cabbages and turnips. Mrs Mckinnon wiped her hands on her apron and poured a cup for Sarah. "Tomorrow, I'll bake some scones," she said. "How would you like that, Elsie?"

Elsie nodded.

"Good."

"Thank you, Mrs Mckinnon," Frances said, looking at the basket of food, "that would be nice."

"I can't wait to sleep in the princess bed," Elsie said, eating her toast.

Frances thought of Elsie's pretty little bed. "When I was a little girl, I'd have loved nothing more than a princess bed," she replied. "You are a very lucky girl, Elsie. Daddy bought this house and decided that you would have a princess bed. How lucky you are."

"Maybe Daddy is a king."

"Maybe he is."

"And Mummy is a queen."

Frances brought the cup to her lips and, in a moment of absentmindedness, scalded her top lip on the tea. She flinched and licked her lip, lowering the cup back down to the table. As she blew tendrils of steam away from it, she noticed something laced around the inside of the china cup: it looked like a crack. She blew some more until it was safe to investigate with a finger. On closer inspection, she saw a long thread of dark brown hair with amber flecks that caught the fading light of the sun. Sarah, who had been watching in horror, apologised. "I didn't see, ma'am."

Frances looked around at her daughter and Sarah. Sarah's mousy, light brown hair was tied up in a braid; mother and daughter were blonde. Mrs Mckinnon's hair was unquestionably grey.

Later that evening, Frances came to say goodnight to Elsie in the nursery. When she reached the top step of the landing, she smiled at the sound of Elsie's little voice, deep in conversation. Frances crept around the corner to see if she could catch a glimpse of the imaginary discussion, as she always enjoyed doing. Elsie was talking to a teddy bear on her bed. Sarah was on the other side of the room folding clothes into a drawer.

"It's time to go to sleep, Finn," she heard her daughter say to the bear. "There's nothing to be afraid of."

Frances' stomach sank with sadness at the thought of anyone being afraid of the dark. She wondered if the bear was acting as a vessel for her daughter's worries and decided to step in. "Nobody's afraid of the dark in here, are they?"

Elsie shook her head. "Finn was, but he's not any more."

"I'm glad to hear it, Finn." Frances looked down at the tatty golden bear in her daughter's arms.

"Mummy," Elsie began, "are you afraid of the dark?"

"No, darling. I'm not afraid of the dark."

"Mary is."

"Is she?"

"Yes. The dark is when she's alone."

Frances' and Sarah's eyes met, locking for a moment. Sarah feigned a smile and said, "I'm sure Mary will be fine, Elsie. Don't worry about such things." She closed the drawer and came to the bedside. "Give your Mummy a kiss and say goodnight. We have church tomorrow, don't forget. A piano lesson, too."

Frances leaned in and kissed Elsie's forehead. "Goodnight sweetheart."

"Goodnight, Mummy."

Frances nodded to Sarah and left the room, closing the nursery door behind her. The sconces on the landing flickered slightly with the backdraft of the closed door, casting long, erratic shadows across the walls.

The dark is when she's alone.

Frances shook her head. "Childish nonsense," she whispered to herself.

She descended the staircase and shot a look across her shoulder despite herself. The landing was still, with a sliver of golden light stretching from underneath the nursery door. She went downstairs in silence.

4

FRANCES WASN'T SURE WHAT time it was when she awoke to the muffled sound of Elsie talking to Sarah upstairs. She pulled a robe over her nightgown and crept up to the top floor to see her. When she opened the door, she found that she was walking into an early morning tea party. A selection of dolls and bears sat around a picnic of tin teapots, plates, cups and saucers. Elsie was talking to Finn again when she noticed her mother standing in the room.

"Good morning," she said, kneeling down to kiss Elsie on the head. "Is there room for me?" Elsie nodded. Frances sat down beside a doll she recognised: Blissy. It looked up at her as usual, with an expressionless, wide-eyed face as only a doll could. Frances, deciding to focus on something else, looked over to the alcove which led to Sarah's room. "Good morning, Sarah," she said, a little louder than how she'd greeted Elsie. There was no response.

"Sarah is downstairs," Elsie said, pouring an imaginary cup of tea for her mother. The tea set was one of the only possessions Elsie had brought with her, shipped as a birthday gift from London on behalf of her father, a year before.

"Is she? I thought I heard you talking to her?"

"I was talking to Mary."

Frances looked around at the dolls to see which one could be Mary. Without their distinct hair colours, they all looked the same; they were bland, with white faces and thick black eyelashes. "Which one is Mary?" she asked, pointing at the sea of shining faces.

"Mary isn't a doll, Mummy." Elsie looked up at her with a patronising tilt of her head. "Mary is a lady, like you."

A sudden, loud clap caused Frances to jump and drop the cup onto the picnic blanket. It was the cuckoo clock, sending a chirping mechanical bird out into the room, flapping its blue wings and dipping its body up and down. It was seven o' clock.

"Oh, Mrs Mckinnon is probably making breakfast. We must get ready for church," Frances said, swiftly departing from the tea party. "Please get dressed."

In the bathroom of the first floor, John was shaving in the mirror as Frances passed. He was naked from the waist up with a face covered in shaving soap. "The moustache isn't going to church?" she asked, watching him gently slide the blade across his top lip, stopping to perform small, precise scrapes under his nose. He rinsed the razor in the sink and started the process again.

"It'll grow back if I change my mind." His reflection winked at her. She leaned on the door frame.

"I think I liked it. It will look rather interesting, that white mouth against a tanned face."

"I'll just have to tan there, too." The blade gleamed in the light of the morning sun as it glided up his neck and the outline of his jaw bone, exposing his skin that had briefly hidden under the white mask. "We had some fine weather last week. Perhaps it will carry on this week."

"Chance would be a fine thing."

"Indeed it would," he said, smiling. His hands looked like long, tan gloves against his white torso.

"You look like a butcher," she remarked.

"A butcher?" he asked, raising his eyebrows ironically. "I thought this was what they call a farmer's tan," he said, flashing a grin. "You say such mean-spirited things to me, Frances. I'll have to whip you." He fixed his gaze on her as she held onto the door frame. She laughed and quickly ran across the landing. The razor clattered in the sink as he discarded it and chased after her.

They met their neighbours and the local vicar at the church. The Swinsons from number seven greeted them in earnest, making the biggest impression on Frances out of all the other parishioners, but not for the best reasons. Edward Swinson informed them several times that he was a doctor, belonging to a surgery on Duke Street. Frances' cheeks ached from the repeated smiles as he spoke. Although he was a friendly man, with a white, neatly trimmed beard and a comically red, bulbous nose, the Bryant's felt that Dr Swinson would have continued speaking had they been there or not. At one point, Frances felt that they were the last people on earth, enduring the aftermath of letting everyone else escape a meeting with Dr Swinson.

In the several attempts at finding an escape with her eyes, Frances had clocked Mrs Swinson—a woman in her fifties, who eyed the Bryant's with a keen, interrogative stare. "You all seem so familiar!" she said, looking down over a hooked nose. Frances laughed nervously and looked up at John who was smiling and putting his hat on.

"That's not possible, unless you are also from West Derby?" she asked. Mrs Swinson shook her head.

"We're from Manchester, originally," she said, fastening her jacket. "We moved here five years ago to open the new surgery. Are you registered with a doctor?"

I will be if I die from boredom today, Frances thought.

"Not yet. Perhaps we should register with you!" John suggested. The Swinsons laughed heartily, and Dr Swinson handed him a card which he took gratefully. She thought he was the most wonderful, patient man in the world as he laughed with them and shook their hands.

"Well, I'm a family doctor, if ever you need one." Dr Swinson looked down at little Elsie who was clutching a doll in her arms. "Or if Polly dolly should ever get sick," he said with a wink. Elsie turned the doll around to show him Emmie, her golden-haired porcelain doll. "She looks like she's in good health, though. What a good nurse you must be!"

They descended the church steps together and stopped in the churchyard that separated the church from their street. Sarah and Elsie walked ahead and sat down on a bench nearby. The Swinsons bade their farewells to the remaining clergy and shuffled across the cobbles back to their home on Percy Street. John watched them walk away and, leaning into his wife's ear, quietly said, "he is a doctor, you know." Frances covered her mouth with a gloved hand and looked at the floor.

"He didn't ask you a single thing about yourself," she observed.

"They think they already know us. Did you catch Mrs Swinson's stare?"

"Yes. I thought she was going to reveal that she was a neighbour from home."

"I did, too. She wouldn't take her eyes off me," he said, adjusting his hat.

"Perhaps she thinks you're a filthy criminal who escaped from the Australian prison camp."

"How do you know I didn't?" he asked with a wink.

"Stop it. Imagine the scandal," she said, half-flushed. "There's enough of that in the papers."

"What do you want to do today, anyway?" he asked, changing the subject. The river snaked in the distance, its scales catching the light of the mid-morning sun. "What do people around here do on Sundays when they don't have front steps to wash?"

5

AFTER A WALK AROUND their new neighbourhood, husband and wife returned home to hear Elsie's light tinkling on the piano trickling into the hall. Each note was clumsy and erratic but when Frances peered around the open doorway, her heart melted at the sight of her daughter's face, fixed in concentration. On several occasions, Sarah had to ask her to tuck her tongue back in during practice. Frances smiled and thought of how she would almost chew on her tongue when focusing too hard on things. Lucky for her, it was beaten out of her by her mother. She hoped that for Elsie's sake, no such action would be required.

The keys started and abruptly stopped each time Elsie forgot the next sequence. Frances giggled silently, remembering her own early piano lessons, for it was no secret that she was terrible for a few years. She thought that at four, Elsie was already showing more promise.

"Shall we try now, Elsie?" asked Sarah. Elsie nodded and waited for Sarah to count down. When it was time, she enthusiastically tapped the first few keys and looked up at Sarah for reassurance. Sarah nodded and gestured for her to carry on.

She did as she was instructed and played *Twinkle Twinkle Little Star*.

When the little girl had finished playing, Frances fluttered into the room with applause. "Bravo, Elsie!" she said, sitting down in a nearby chair.

"Shall I do it again?" Elsie asked, turning around in the seat. Frances nodded vehemently. "Play all day, if you like. It's wonderful."

Elsie began to play again with more confidence, singing along in a tiny, pleasant voice. Frances and Sarah watched and smiled with encouragement as Elsie played, until their reverie was broken with the sharp thud of something on the window. Elsie saw it first.

Frances approached the glass with horror, taking stock of the blood smears on the pane. She looked down at the patio to see a crumpled blackbird on the flag stones. Elsie let out a high-pitched scream.

For a moment, Frances felt everything in the room fall back into a muffled quietude, cooling her to the bone. She couldn't take her eyes off the blood. Almost in the blink of an eye, Elsie's screams vibrated through her skull and brought her back into the scene.

"Take her into the kitchen, Sarah. I'll get John to clean it up," Frances said, ushering them out of the room. She returned to the window and looked down at the unfortunate creature; it was mangled.

"What's going on in here?" John asked, rushing into the room. Frances didn't say anything. She simply moved away from the glass and let him see for himself. "Good God," he said, covering his grimace with his hand. "That's a bird? It flew into the window?"

"I know."

They both looked down at the cluster of black feathers caked in blood.

Mrs Mckinnon found Frances sitting at the piano later that afternoon, staring at a discoloured patch where the bird had once been. John had dutifully cleaned it up and disposed of it, desperately trying not to retch in front of his wife as he did so, but the small stain remained, haunting her. For reasons that she couldn't explain, she couldn't remove her eyes from the spot. She didn't want to look at it, but she felt she had no choice. She thought of the creature's broken body, twisted in an unnatural way, as though the pitiful thing had been mutilated before being thrown at the window, just to frighten her.

The window had since been opened, allowing the cacophony of the outside world to come in. Birds sang in the trees overhead as though nothing had happened. Frances remained still.

The drawing room door was wide open, so it surprised Frances to hear a gentle knock. "I know it's my day off, Ma'am, but I hope you don't mind me bringing you some tea." Mrs Mckinnon's soft voice seemed to rouse her from her fixation.

Frances looked up at the housekeeper with sleepy eyes. "I don't mind at all, Mrs Mckinnon. Thank you." She took a small cup from the tray and moved over to sit at the table. She sank into the chair and held the cup close to her with both hands.

"And the wee one, ma'am... She was so upset. I had to do something. I made her some buns."

Frances' bottom lip trembled. "Thank you."

Mrs Mckinnon placed the tray down at the table and sat beside Frances. "You know, these things aren't always omens, ma'am."

Taken aback, Frances straightened in the chair. "How did you...?"

Mrs Mckinnon gave a knowing nod. "I come from a long line of superstitious people too, ma'am. Fairies, vampires—ach—I've heard it all. I don't mean to say none of it's true, ma'am. I just mean that with such a nice family as yours is, you needn't worry yourself."

Frances looked down at Mrs Mckinnon's gentle hand resting on top of hers. She hadn't noticed it until now. It felt like the hand of an old friend. "Thank you," she said. "It was horrible."

"I'm sure it was! Not something a child should see."

"It was so mangled. I've never seen anything like it."

"I bet it was an escapee, straight from the cat's claws. Flew into the window and had a swift, merciful death."

"Perhaps." Frances stared into nowhere. "Perhaps it was nothing, just as you say," she said quietly.

"You just let me know if there's anything else I can do. I'd left some cold cuts for your supper but I might have to make something hot to warm these hands!" she said, holding both of Frances' cold hands in hers. "You'd think it was December in here."

"I don't think I'm feeling well," Frances admitted. "This house has been so..." she thought for a moment. Finding herself unaccustomed to running a household staff, Frances wasn't sure if she should tell Mrs Mckinnon anything. If she were being honest with herself, she actually felt that Mrs Mckinnon would think her insane. She bit her bottom lip and looked away. "Oh it doesn't matter."

"As long as you're sure, ma'am," Mrs Mckinnon said, looking over low-resting spectacles. It felt like an offer. Frances, as much as she wanted to blurt out the words,, *I feel like an imposter. I bumble around this enormous house without any cleaning or cooking to do and I don't want to touch anything because it doesn't feel like it's mine*, knew better than to bare her soul to someone she didn't know. Mrs Mckinnon was warm and approachable, but Frances felt that unloading her emotional baggage onto the woman was a step too far.

"I think I need to rest," she eventually said. She rose from the table and stumbled, struggling to steady herself with a light head. Mrs Mckinnon quickly grabbed an arm and helped her to balance. "I'm so sorry, I don't feel very well," she mumbled.

"Let's get you to bed then, ma'am. I'll bring your tea up."

They walked to the foot of the stairs where, on feeling more able to stand, Frances reached out and grabbed the handrail. She gingerly took her first step, placing her left foot forward, then slowly allowed the right foot to meet it. The gentle hand on her back reassured her that she wouldn't fall, and it stayed with her for the duration. Gradually increasing her speed until she was at her normal pace for climbing stairs, Frances was relieved to see the light of her bedroom illuminating the landing. The door was open wide with her bed waiting for her in her line of sight. She felt incredibly guilty when she heard laboured breathing behind her.

"Thank you, Mrs Mckinnon, I can manage from—" She turned to find that nobody was standing behind her.

"Did you say something, dear?" Mrs Mckinnon called from the foot of the stairs. "I just went back for the tea. I'll be up in a moment."

6

FEELING THE COOL, STICKY sweat of her body clinging to her nightgown, Frances removed the blanket and turned over, hoping to find a more comfortable temperature. It was no use. The room felt airless; the bed felt wet. She shuffled uncomfortably for a few minutes more. Her hair, matted and damp, stuck to her face as she tossed and turned.

"My darling Frances, just how long are you going to stay in this bed?" she heard her husband ask. Opening one eye, she could make out his silhouette on the edge of the bed.

"John?" she asked with a dry mouth. "What time is it?" She could sense that it was light outside, but as to whether it was dusk or dawn, she had no idea.

"What *day* it is, rather," he said. "It's Tuesday morning. You've been sleeping, babbling and wandering for two days."

She stretched and sat up, pushing her long, tangled web of blonde hair away from her face. She couldn't quite believe how long she'd slept for. "I have?" she asked with a yawn.

"You have. I've been sleeping on that wretched chaise lounge with one eye open so you don't wander off the bloody balcony or something." His shirt was heavily creased and unbuttoned at the neck, revealing some of his chest hair. His shirt, rolled up at the sleeves, contrasted with his strong golden forearms. He had dark circles underneath his eyes and, clearly having been too occupied to maintain other daily rituals, looked unkempt, with his stubble casting a shadow across his jaw, darkening right where the cleft in the middle of his chin was.

"Oh dear," she said, scratching her head. The balcony of interest was a decorative feature outside their bedroom window. Having had a look at the wrought iron structure of it, she had previously decided that it was too flimsy to sit out on and instead resolved to pretend that it wasn't there. "We're quite high up," she said, looking over at the open window. "I don't know what I was doing over there. I have always despised heights."

"And that's not the worst part. No other than our dear friend Dr Swinson has been doing house calls. That man can talk for England—sorry darling—this really is none of your concern right now." He patted her leg. "I shouldn't add to your malaise like that."

"That's all right. Perhaps it was Dr Swinson that kept me asleep," she said, sipping from a glass of water that had been stationed at her bedside. John belly laughed at the edge of the bed.

"God I've missed you."

"I'm sorry to have worried you."

"Are you feeling better?"

"Yes. I'm tired, though. Very tired."

"He's coming again at lunch time and his fee—well, I'll end up paying him with a cob of coal by the end of the week, ha! Would you like some breakfast? I can send Mrs Mckinnon up?"

"I probably should."

John stretched across the bed and kissed her on the forehead; his closeness caused her to recoil slightly. As conscious as she was of her damp nightgown and sweaty face, he didn't seem to mind. He winked and headed downstairs to the kitchen. Frances slowly rolled out of the bed and wandered toward the bathroom.

Maggie was leaving just as she arrived. The girl bowed slightly, speaking in her timid voice as she said, "morning, ma'am. I hope that you're feeling better."

"Thanks, Maggie," she said. Young Maggie had a cloth in her hand and popped it into the bucket that sat just outside the door, as though discarding incriminating evidence from her mistress.

"I-I've just finished cleaning it, ma'am. W-would you like me t-to run you a bath?"

Frances, having only ever washed at the washstand, thought about it for a moment.

"That would be lovely, Maggie. I would like a bath."

Maggie nodded and returned to the bathroom. "I'll let you know when it's ready, ma'am," she said. Frances returned to her bedroom and stood at the window, hoping that the breeze would ease the stickiness between her skin and the fabric on her body. The world outside was silent for a moment.

Mrs Mckinnon bustled into the bedroom with a tray of break-fast items and coffee. "Good morning ma'am," she said happily. "I can't tell you how glad we are to see you up and about." She laid the tray down on the side table and uncovered the plate of boiled eggs and ham. "Mr Bryant wasn't sure what you'd like, so I've given you a bit of everything... and I can make you some beef tea to help you get your strength up, if none of this will do." She poured out a small cup of coffee and walked over to Frances, holding it out like it was the elixir of life.

Frances took it gently and thanked her. "I'm sorry to have troubled everybody."

"Ach, say no more of it. It's our job to take good care of you."

"Thank you, Mrs Mckinnon."

As the old lady headed to the doorway, Frances couldn't help but ask about the other night. The poor woman looked bemused when Frances asked her about the hand on her back. She seemed to stiffen, brushing her hands against her apron.

"I don't know what you mean, ma'am? I helped you to the bottom step," she said, frowning. "You said you were happy to take it from there, so I went back to get the tea. I should think you were feeling rather unwell... would you like me to call Dr Swinson?"

"No, thank you, Mrs Mckinnon. It must have been a fever dream."

"Aye, ma'am. We all get them, I'm sure!"

"That's all it was, yes," Frances admitted, looking down at the cup. "It could have been one of *many* dreams I've had over the past two days. Thank you, Mrs Mckinnon. That will be all for now."

She watched the old woman leave, suspicion growing steadily in her gut.

7

BEATRICE LARKIN ARRIVED JUST after lunch on the Wednesday morning following Frances' brief illness. On greeting her daughter in the hallway with a swift kiss on the cheek, Mrs Larkin's first remark was about the ghostly paleness of her face. "You look dreadful, my dear." She allowed Maggie to take her coat and hat and hang them up, briefly acknowledging the girl and immediately turning her attention back to Frances.

"I have been unwell," Frances said firmly.

"You should have sent for me."

"I was asleep for most of it."

"John should have sent for me then."

"Perhaps," Frances agreed, "but it is all in hand."

"It's terribly lonely in that cottage with you and the little one gone. Don't ever think you can't send for me."

"I won't, I promise."

"Where is your husband, anyway?" She craned her neck to look around the large, empty hallway.

"He is out at a business meeting. He will be back for dinner."

Beatrice tilted her head, casting her heavy-lidded eyes down her stern face. "And my granddaughter?"

"She will be back in an hour. She is still out at the park."

Beatrice harrumphed. "Did *anybody* know that I was coming?"

"Of course. John is working. I thought we could have some tea together first."

She seemed pleased by the suggestion and followed her daughter into the parlour room where Mrs Mckinnon had just laid a tray of tea and cakes out. Frances hadn't seen her pass, but the teapot was hot to the touch.

"This is a fine house, Frances," she said matter of factly as she sat down on the sofa and studied the decor with raised eyebrows. "I must say, I am impressed."

Impressed by what, Mother? The fact that John isn't the cur you thought he was? Frances decided not to bite and instead, smiled at her mother as she poured tea into two china cups. "Thank you. It still feels like a dream to me."

"I'll say. You must be rubbing shoulders with the gentry out here." Beatrice plopped two cubes of sugar into her cup and stirred until she had a little terracotta whirlpool in her hands.

"Not quite. At least, I haven't met any of the sort," Frances said, passing her the milk jug.

Beatrice dropped no more than a splash into her cup and placed the small white jug back on the tray. "Have you met your neighbours?"

"Some of them," Frances shrugged. "We have a doctor, a couple of businessmen and a solicitor. That's who I've met so far at church."

"What's the church like?"

"St Bride's? It's very good."

"Looks like a pagan temple to me—don't slouch, Frances."

"I suppose it does, yes." Frances, straightening, focused on her drink and desperately thought of something else that they could talk about. "Would you like me to give you a tour of the house?" she asked, not really wanting to move. She still felt exhausted.

"I'd expect nothing less, dear girl," Beatrice said with a wide smile.

As they toured the Percy Street home, Beatrice, unable to disguise her delight at the grandness of the house, made several approving noises accompanied by the occasional "oo" and "ahh" as she inspected ornaments and brushed her fingers across surfaces. "Isn't it grand?" she asked at what seemed to Frances, every time they reached the next yard's worth of house. Frances nodded as she silently waited in the hallway for Beatrice to come and see the bedrooms.

Her mother stopped at the window of the master bedroom and eyed the church across the street. "It's just a bit... different isn't it?"

Frances came to the window and looked down at the stone pillars that fronted the white building. "Yes, but it's still a church inside. It has its pews and things, you know, all the bells and whistles you'd expect."

Beatrice let out an approving grunt and turned on her heel. "I take it the nursery is upstairs?"

As soon as she had fixed her eyes on the nursery, Beatrice gushed. "Oh, Frances," Beatrice said with her hands on her face, "it's delightful." Beatrice walked along the row of dolls and tapped the rocking horse. "How lovely."

Frances, relaxing a little, sat down on Elsie's princess bed and watched her mother flit about the room, fiddling with toys and nosing out of the window. Frances, knowing that the view from Elsie's window was no different to the view from her window downstairs, rolled her eyes slightly. "It's only the same view, you know," she said.

"I know. Lovely though isn't it?" Beatrice moved away from the window, crossed the room and stopped suddenly at the wardrobe on the partition wall, rubbing her arms as though she'd walked through a draught. "Cold over here."

"Is it?"

Beatrice looked down at the section of floor that was warmed by the afternoon sun and shook her head. "Yes," she said, turning to look at her daughter. "Like there's a door open." Frances looked around, feeling nothing.

"There's only one door. Sarah sleeps in there," she said, pointing to the alcove that divided the room. Beatrice stepped into the space.

"Warm in here."

Frances wanted to retreat. "How odd. Shall we go back downstairs?"

"Just a moment," Beatrice said, sticking her nose behind the wardrobe. "It's cold behind here."

"Please don't," Frances said. "We should go back downstairs. John can move it. Please don't hurt yourself."

Beatrice withdrew from her investigation and followed her silently out of the room, casting a look behind her in case of surprises.

"How long has John had this house?" she asked calmly, standing at the foot of the third floor staircase.

"Only a few months. Why?"

"How old is it?"

"I don't really know. Ten years or so?"

"Hmm," her mother said, folding her arms.

"What is it?"

"Probably nothing, my love." She shook it off. "Probably nothing."

Later, after Beatrice had played with Elsie and insisted on helping Sarah to tidy up the toys, she came downstairs to dinner. Mrs Mckinnon had provided ample food for their special guest. "Well it's just lovely. Thank you so much for having me," Beatrice said, laying a napkin on her lap.

"You are welcome, Beatrice," John said, raising a glass. As he settled into his thirties, John Bryant was devastatingly handsome, even more so in a dinner jacket. Frances watched him charm her mother from across the table and smirked. Beatrice seldom had any words to say to her son-in-law outside of civil pleasantries, but she couldn't get away with not smiling every now and then. He was magnetic.

"You are looking very lovely, Beatrice," he said.

"Thank you, dear. I must say, I do love the house. You've done so well, young man."

"It is the least Frances deserves, I should think," he said.

Frances held her breath for a moment. There was, and she felt always would be, an awkwardness when it came to talking about her marriage, and his absence soon after Elsie's birth. Frances, although now civil and in want of a relationship with her mother, still bore the emotional scars of her parents disowning her at twenty-one, when she ran off with John Bryant, a common farm labourer. Since she had met him, he had gone on to find his fortune first in the Australian wool trade and secondly, as a prospector. Her father, the vicar of the local parish, hadn't approved of John's proposal, and wanted him hanged for taking his daughter to Gretna Green in the summer of 1886.

Unbeknownst to both Reverend Edmund Larkin and John himself, days before proposing to Frances, he had inherited a small amount of money originally intended for his late mother—an illegitimate daughter of the otherwise childless landowner she had worked for. She died several years before the will had been enacted, leaving everything to her only surviving child, John. Frances felt it was more than ironic how the boy with noble blood was spurned by her parents, yet hosted her mother at his table as though she were his own.

There was no need for Frances to fear. Beatrice agreed and, almost tearing up as she said it, declared that "you have given her the world, and for that I am grateful, John. I could not have wished for more from a son."

He had done it. After years of hard labour both in the gold-fields and in the conversations with Beatrice Larkin, he had done it. Frances sipped her wine and smiled. All would be well.

Later that night, Frances showed her mother to the guest room. Beatrice, having indulged herself in John's tour of the drinks cabinet, adjusted her affections accordingly and squeezed her daughter in an embrace only a mother could give.

"Ring the bell if you need anything from Maggie or Mrs Mckinnon," Frances said breathlessly.

"I shall. But you must tell me something, and be truthful."

"What is it?"

Beatrice stepped back and held Frances' shoulders, looking into her face searchingly. "Do you believe this house to be haunted?"

"What? What do you mean?"

"Greenwood women have the sense, Frances. I thought it had skipped a generation with you but... but now I'm not so sure."

Frances shook her head. "I don't... I... haunted? Do you believe that?" She thought of the bird, the ornaments, the dolls, the dresses, the errant hair in the teacup, the sense that she wasn't in her own home. Her chest tightened. "Mary," she said.

"Who?"

"Elsie said something about someone called Mary. She said 'Mary isn't a doll, Mummy. She's a lady,' and I know that a small child can have a wild imagination but she said it with such conviction." Frances shuddered. *The dark is when she's alone.*

"Well," Beatrice began, brushing her skirts, "if you need me to *do anything*, you know that you simply have to send for me and I will be here."

"That won't be necessary—"

"I have been back to that nursery, Frances. Something is amiss in there. Sarah can't sense it, else she would have told you. Elsie certainly can. That child has seen things." The intensity in Beatrice's face made Frances think before uttering her next words.

Unable to deny it, Frances dropped her shoulders with a deep sigh. "Last night," she said, "I wasn't feeling very well and Mrs McKinnon—well, I thought it was her anyway—Mrs Mckinnon helped me up the stairs. Then I turned around and she wasn't there. She was still in the drawing room. I felt a hand on my back and someone breathing heavily behind me."

Beatrice, who had sobered at some point during the conversation, looked at her with wide eyes.

"What else has happened?"

"Well, nothing yesterday but... I don't know, this house, it..."

"Tell me again. Do you suspect that it's haunted?"

Frances, alarmed at her mother's concerned directness, straightened. "Haunted?"

Beatrice nodded. "You said about the bird, then the hand on the back, then the breathing. Tell me, Frances, do you think your home is haunted?"

The word escaped out of Frances' mouth before she could even think about her response: "Yes."

8

FRANCES LAY AWAKE FOR some time before John came to bed. He had strongly encouraged his mother in law to sample the drinks cabinet with him and as a result, was also incredibly happy to see Frances.

Whether it was the alcohol or the fact that they were still readjusting to living together, his body seemed strange to her, almost as though she hadn't touched it before. Every time he touched her, she felt a buzz of electricity. "My mother is in the next room," she whispered as he kissed her neck.

"I know. Makes it all the more exciting, eh?"

Any response she had thought to give had been reduced to a small gasp. She couldn't refuse him.

His sinewy back muscles tensed as she writhed beneath him. Her body recorded every tender kiss that landed, making their marks on long-forgotten territory like lashings of rain on the sleek pavement outside. She fantasised then that she didn't really know him; this made her enjoy the moment all the more.

When they were finally too tired to go on, she lay in his arms and listened to his heartbeat.

"What was it like in Australia?" she asked casually.

"Hard work."

"I can only imagine."

"And let's keep it that way. I don't want these beautiful hands to ever harden." He held her hands in his and kissed them. "I thought about you every day."

"As I did you."

"I even named a sheep after you."

"John!" she slapped his chest and rolled out of bed, slipping her nightgown back over her body.

"I'm teasing," he said with a deep, dry chuckle. "Although, some of the types I've met definitely would have... you know..." He raised an eyebrow.

"Oh, that's disgusting."

"Hardly any women out there."

"Really?" She curled up beside him and rested her head on his chest. He knew why she was asking. The tinge of disbelief in her voice betrayed her feigned indifference.

"Frances Elizabeth Bryant, you listen here," he began, "Queensland could have been the capital of the entire female population and there would be *none*, not a single one, that could turn my head the way you do."

She laughed.

"I mean it. I counted down the days until I could come back to you." She looked up at him. "It's rough out there. I wanted nothing more than to be here, but not until I could secure our future." He brushed her hair away from her forehead. "I used the money that had been left to me to buy passage to Brisbane and a decent sized flock. Twelve months on, I was selling wool to Japan. The money earned itself after a time. A friend encouraged me to get out into the goldfields and... well—your bit of rough's a gentleman now, 'owd you like that?"

"How did you come by the house?"

"It's not the most interesting of stories, but it was an elderly gent called Mr Ellman, who owns the shipping company. He sold it to me on the way home. Why all the questions, anyway, are you not tired any more?" he asked, stroking the outline of her hip with a finger, "because you just say the word and—" She laughed again and pushed him off.

"I am tired. I suppose I just wondered if you wanted to talk about it."

"I swear to you, it was mostly uneventful." She studied his eyes once more. She sighed and realised that if there were any lies hiding there, she would never find them.

After extinguishing the lamp at her bedside, she slipped down under the covers and leaned in to him, drifting off to sleep in his warmth.

Her sleepiness didn't last. Frances tossed and turned all night, finally waking when she felt tiny, cold splashes on her face. She lay on her back and opened her eyes, looking into the pitch blackness. It took a few moments for her eyes to adjust to the darkness, but the ceiling seemed as white as always. The curtains had been left open, letting the moonlight peer in. The shadows seemed longer, darker, more ominous. She looked up again to see a small black circle, widening with every blink. The splashes grew heavier, landing in her eyes and on her lips. She wiped them away with the back of her hand, only to find more to take the place of those that had been smeared. She sat up and reached for the matches in the bedside drawer; she lit the lamp on her bedside table.

While she adjusted the intensity of the flame, the circle on the ceiling above her head was growing wider, losing its shape and spilling into a shadowy pool that began to gush. She felt it trickling down her back, soaking her nightgown. She turned around to look at it. It was blood.

John woke to the sound of his wife screaming in the corner of the room. "Fan! What's wrong?" he asked, almost shaking her. She pointed to the ceiling.

"Blood. There was so much blood!"

He looked in the direction of where she was pointing and shook his head. The ceiling was white, as were the blankets on the bed. He went over to them and smoothed his hands over the sheets. "They're dry," he assured her. She stood up and followed him to the bed. "Come back to bed. You've had a bad dream."

She lay down once more and looked up at the ceiling. There was nothing there.

9

BEATRICE BROUGHT THE BREAKFAST tray to Frances' bed-side the following morning. "John said you'd been up with nightmares," she said, placing the tray of breakfast items on the side table. She picked up a pewter mug and turned to face her daughter.

"Mother, Mrs Mckinnon—"

"Isn't your mother. Now sit up and drink some beef tea."

Frances did as she was told. She took the tea and blew on it, inhaling the strong, savoury scent.

"For strength and beauty," Beatrice said, sitting down on the chair beside the bed. "I'm due to go back after lunch, unless you would like me to stay awhile longer?"

Frances shook her head. "It was a bad dream and no more."

"Have you been saying your prayers before bed?"

"Always," Frances said, sipping some beef broth from the mug. Beatrice pursed her lips and looked around the room. "So, have you seen anything that would indicate who this Mary character is?"

"No." Frances shook her head. "I haven't *seen* anything..."

Beatrice eyed her suspiciously. "What was the nightmare about? Boggarts? Spring-heeled Jack?" she asked with an eyebrow raised. Frances shrugged.

"Frances, you're a terrible liar."

"There was blood, all right? It was coming from the ceiling and dripping all over me."

Frances was surprised to see that this information did not cause her mother to grimace. Instead, Beatrice leaned in, listening intently.

"Interesting."

"Is it?"

Beatrice's eyes lit up. "I know a man, you know. He's a clairvoyant."

"Oh, Mother, really—"

"No, no, I promise you—he's a good man. He was the organist at church, you might remember him. Trevor Kingsley. The postman?"

"Mr Kingsley's a clairvoyant?"

Beatrice nodded, "and a very good one at that. He helped Mrs Lindsay find her missing keys. Her husband was a gatekeeper, God rest his soul. He misplaced the only set of keys for the gatehouse on the night he died. Mrs Lindsay managed to find them down a ginnel thanks to Richard."

Frances blinked at her mother. Beatrice, as far as Frances had known, believed in God and the Devil but had never, not once in her lifetime, indicated that she believed in ghosts. "I see," was all she could say, sipping her tea.

"I know it sounds, well you know... but really, I think we could do a seance here and get to the bottom of it. It's unusual for such a young house to have spirits rattling around in it. You just never know."

"Indeed." Frances rolled her eyes and reached for a bread roll. "Where's Elsie?"

"Oh she's doing some lessons downstairs with Sarah. Sarah is ever so good, you know."

I know, Mother. It was me who appointed her in the first place, after all. "She is," Frances agreed. Sarah had been the light in the darkest of tunnels, cradling Elsie to sleep in the early days while Frances sobbed into her handkerchief and mourned the absence of her husband, her family and her life as a single woman. Sarah was the sister Frances never had. Nothing was ever too much trouble. At times, Frances felt she was being ridiculous, having a nanny care for her own child, but she remembered that it had been John's insistence that she had had help at home in the first place. He had no mother or sisters to help and nor did she. "I hope the day never comes when she says she wants to leave," she said.

"Well, she is a vicar's daughter, much like yourself. I'm sure she'll make a fine governess, just as you would have done."

Frances prickled. "School teachers are different, mother." Frances' parents had expected her to teach into her mid-twenties, eventually leaving the profession in order to marry someone they deemed suitable for an educated child of a clergyman.

Even the mention of schooling was too tender a wound for Frances. "I was never a governess."

"Yes, but you know what I mean."

"Yes." Frances tore at her roll and stuffed the chunks of bread into her mouth, chewing them slowly. Beatrice, having finally acknowledged her unsuitable choice of conversation, lifted herself out of the chair and started plumping cushions and making the bed with vigour. Frances, seeing that it was time to get up, reached for her slippers and walked to the wardrobe. "I need to dress, Mother."

"I'll be out of your hair in a moment," Beatrice said, beating the last of the pillows with a resounding thump. "There. Marvellous—oh? Are these all yours?" she asked, looking over at the wardrobe that Frances had just opened.

"Yes, I... I think so. They're new."

Beatrice walked closer to the wardrobe and slid the hangers to the side one by one, admiring the skirts and embellishments of the gowns. "Well," she said with thin lips. "There's a lot of money in gold, it seems." Frances blushed, not knowing what to do as she watched her mother inspect the clothing, audibly gasping at the silk ribbons.

"Oh, you're up and about!" John said, standing in the doorway. Beatrice, as though caught rifling through a stranger's intimate possessions, bolted upright and tidied her greying gold hair.

"These are very beautiful dresses, Frances. I'm going downstairs." She gave a quick nod and slid out of the bedroom past John, quietly offering a 'good morning' as she passed.

"Good morning Beatrice," he said with a nod.

"John," Frances asked, failing to find the words for the rest of her question.

As though he had read her mind, he smiled. "It's about the dresses, isn't it?"

"Yes. Where did you get them?"

His mouth straightened. "All right... they came with the house." Frances stared at him as he spoke. "They looked like they were about your size and I thought it would be a pity to throw them out... they look like they're worth a few bob."

"They came with the house?" Frances could feel her heart throbbing in her throat. He rushed over and caught her before she fell to the floor.

"Frances, what's wrong?"

"I... I just, I need to sit down." He helped her to the bed and lifted her legs up onto the mattress.

"What is it? Don't you like them? It's fine, I'll get shut of them, Christ, why are you so pale?"

"John, whose dresses are these?"

He shrugged. "I don't know. Nobody asked for them back so I just assumed that, once the contracts were signed, they belonged to me as they were left here."

"John, their previous owner could be dead!"

"Frances, I'm really struggling to see what the issue is. You can buy second hand frocks at the market, can't you?" He shook his head in bafflement. "How is this any different?"

"It just *is*." She held a hand to her mouth as her bottom lip trembled. "I don't know what to do with them." She wiped away a couple of tears.

"No need for hysterics, Frances," John said, raising his hands in surrender. "If you want rid of them, that's fine, but can you at least wait until tomorrow?"

"Why? What's tomorrow?"

"I was going to take you out to dinner tonight and if you chuck them today, you won't have a stitch to wear. It'd be good to go out. You haven't left the house since Sunday."

"Dinner?" she asked, dumbfounded.

"Yes. I'd like to take you for dinner, you madwoman. I said Thursday, remember? What do you think about that?"

"I'd love to, but—"

"Shh," he said, placing a finger on her lips. "Stop worrying about it. I'll bet they just belonged to some rich lass who had more than she could wear in a lifetime. Think no more of it." He kissed her on the forehead and stood up, checking his pocket watch. "I have a meeting at ten. I'll see you back here this after-noon." He stopped at the doorway and blew a kiss.

Frances placed her head on the pillow and stared at the ceiling again.

10

ELSIE WAS SITTING ON her bed when Frances came upstairs to say goodnight. "Mummy, you look beautiful," she cried when Frances entered the room in the red gown. It trailed slightly as she walked across to the bed. It was the most elegant dress that she had ever worn and she had spent the entire day altering the bust and the shoulders. The previous owner had possessed a slightly larger frame and a more generously proportioned chest. Frances considered it a blessing that there was half an inch to spare in each seam and dart, else she'd have absolutely nothing to wear.

"Thank you my darling," she said as she sat down on the bed, smoothing her skirts. She caught a glimpse of herself on a table mirror and thought that the rouge complemented her fair skin, almost as though it was made for her. Although she had doused herself with some of her own perfume, there was still a faint scent that she didn't recognise. It wasn't unpleasant—it just wasn't her scent.

She looked over to Elsie who was playing with a music box that Frances hadn't noticed earlier. "This is lovely," her mother said, holding the box in her gloved hands. She wound the brass key until the resistance became too strong for her fingers and let it go. It played a familiar melody. Elsie hummed along.

"Bring back, bring back, oh bring back my bonnie to me, to me," Frances sang quietly. Elsie's eyes lit up.

"Do you know it, Mummy?"

"I do. It's called *My Bonnie.*"

"Is it a sad song?"

"I don't think so."

"How does it go?"

"My Bonnie lies over the ocean,

My Bonnie lies over the sea,

My Bonnie lies over the ocean,

Oh, bring back my Bon- nie to me.

Bring back, bring back,

Oh, bring back my Bon-
nie to me, to me.

Bring back, bring back,

Oh, bring back my Bon-
nie to me."

Elsie, placated with the lullaby, slipped down under her covers. Frances placed the music box on Elsie's bedside table and kissed her forehead. "Sarah is taking care of you while Mummy and Daddy go out. Are you going to be a good girl?"

Elsie nodded happily. "I am always a good girl."

"That you are, sweetheart." She stroked her golden hair and tucked her in, inhaling her daughter's unique smell as she kissed her.

Sarah followed her out to the other side of the door. Elsie watched them leave and rolled over.

"I hope you have a lovely evening, ma'am," Sarah said, admiring the dress. "You look beautiful."

"Thank you Sarah." Frances turned away, grabbed the hand rail and stopped herself. "Just one thing—Sarah. I've noticed that Elsie has been telling little lies since we arrived here."

"Oh?" Sarah closed the bedroom door over so Elsie couldn't hear.

Frances looked around at the empty landing. "It's probably nothing, but you need to keep an eye on her. She says her Daddy didn't buy any of the toys in her room. I don't know why she'd say that, but I'd like it if you could discourage the dishonesty. He must have bought the music box, too. I don't know why she thinks otherwise."

Sarah's brows were knotted in a tangle above her striking green eyes. "I hadn't noticed, ma'am, but I'll keep an eye on her."

"Thank you, Sarah."

John had booked a table at a new hotel less than a five minute ride away from their home. Frances fidgeted with her new satin gloves in the back of the cab as they rode through the street and down towards the city centre. The reassuring clip-clop of hooves helped her steady her breath as she thought of the crowded dining room that awaited them. She had mostly lived a quiet life with her mother on the outskirts; the city, growing larger each year, had always seemed enormous and terrifying.

"You're a sight for sore eyes, stop fidgeting," John said, resting a hand on her lap.

"I'm sorry. I haven't been to dinner in such a long time," she said, looking out of the window. "I'm out of practice." She fiddled with the velvet collar around her neck. It was itching her.

"I'm sorry, darling. It's my fault."

"No, no, This wouldn't be happening if it weren't for you, John." She thought of the house and the money. He was wearing a new dinner suit and top hat. "It's really lovely. I am looking forward to our new life here."

"It's what we deserve," he said.

The maitre d' guided them to their table in the grand dining room. "They have balls here, too," John said with a wink. "Perhaps you'd like to go to a ball one day."

The thought of ballrooms and dancing lightened her head. She had not danced since before they were married—she had been just a girl. She met John at a church fete when she was twenty. He was twenty-five and as far as Beatrice was concerned, must have still been a bachelor for good reason: "can't be unmarried at that age unless there's something wrong with them," she remarked. He would often visit Frances at the schoolhouse, stealing a moment with her on her way home, or meeting her for a walk on the way to work. In the autumn, he would bring her a basket of apples from the nearby orchard, "for my favourite teacher," he'd joke. Every night, her mother would pop her head into Frances' bedroom to make sure that she was exactly where she was supposed to be. Frances knew this, and waited until the light under her mother's bedroom door was dark before slipping out on summer evenings. She fell helplessly, recklessly in love with John Bryant, and she couldn't stand to be away from him.

It was to Beatrice's deepest regret that her daughter had ignored her parents' wishes and married him anyway. They eloped to Gretna Green in September of 1887, returning to West Derby in December of the same year. Her father, too angered to speak to her, held off any communications until he reached his deathbed in 1889. Her mother, now alone and mourning, reached out to her daughter upon her husband's death. The memory filled Frances with shame, flushing her cheeks crimson as she was shown to her seat.

"Are you all right?" John asked, fixing his gaze on her from across the table. She nodded.

"It's warm in here, that's all." She fanned herself with a hand and sipped some water. She looked over to her husband, who was relaxed in the chair with his legs crossed. The restaurant was incredibly busy, even though it was to be expected. She felt her hands shaking as she slowly drank some more water. People were looking at her.

"You're the most beautiful woman in the room, Fan," he said, smiling with even, neat teeth. She blushed again, feeling like a doll on display in a shop window. "The moment I saw you, I just had to have you. I meant to come home sooner, I really did. Australia is just so damn far away."

"Oh, it doesn't matter. You're here now and that's all that matters." She opened the menu and stared at the pages, unable to focus on any particular item.

"Ah, yes," he said with sinking shoulders, "about that." He leaned forward and tugged on his lapel. "I need to go to South Africa a week on Monday," he said in a quiet voice. She barely heard him over the clinking of cutlery, music and conversation from the other diners, but she did hear him, much to her chagrin. She felt her heart sink through her chest. Her hands felt clammy.

"No," was all she could say.

"Not forever. Just for a month or so. There is some business I need to attend to. It's worth quite a lot of money. It's important business." He fixed his beautiful bright eyes on hers. "I promise, it's the last time."

"It'll take more than a month, John," she said, shaking her head.

"Yes, I suppose, what? Three weeks travel either side? More like two and a half months."

She swallowed back tears. "No," she said, her voice wavering with disappointment.

"Frances, it's all right. It's just one trip. That's it."

"Please, you can't leave me." Tears rolled down her cheeks. She quickly grabbed the napkin and dabbed her eyes. "I'm sorry. I'm just so scared, John."

"What? What are you scared of?"

"I don't want to be alone again." She swallowed back tears and stared at him. He looked devastated.

"I promise you, I'm coming back." He reached out to touch her hand.

"Excuse me for a moment." She lifted herself from the chair and sailed out into the foyer, looking for the W.C. The foyer was crowded with dinner guests and tourists loitering and smoking on the sofas. She brushed past them and looked across at a mirror on the wall.

Her heart stopped. In the foreground of the reflection, she saw a chestnut-haired woman, slightly taller than she was, wearing the same red dress. Her scarlet shape provided a stark contrast with the smattering of black and white clad gentlemen in the room behind her. With an expressionless gaze, she looked at Frances, as though studying her for a minute. Frances inhaled a deep breath and held it. The brunette's expression transformed from a look of indifference to sheer terror, and with her mouth rounded and open wide, she let out a piercing scream, shattering the mirror into a thousand pieces. Frances shielded herself from the shards and rolled to the floor.

"Fan?" John was staring at her, waiting for her to respond to his question. She looked around in disbelief; she was sitting back at the dinner table, holding his hand. The music, the chatter and the clinking of cutlery was as it had been before.

"I'm so sorry, what did you say?"

"I said I'm coming back."

"Gold?"

"Yes. They've just opened more goldfields."

"You're going to be prospecting?"

He shook his head and said, "no, I'm just keeping an eye on things. The man who sold me the house, Mr Ellman? Well... I work for him, but he's old. He's too ill to go this time. I've been asked to go in his place."

"Oh... I understand."

He leaned back in his seat, confused by her sudden change of behaviour. "Are you all right?" he finally asked.

"I'm fine. I'm just famished, probably," she said, catching sight of the waiter approaching with the trolley. "Oh look, dinner's here."

11

She gripped his hand tightly on the cab ride home, as though if she held on for long enough, fate would change its mind, and Mr Ellman would be able to go as planned. "I'm going to be back in no time," John said.

"I know. I know."

"Your mother will be pleased."

"No she won't. She's fond of you now."

"Even more fond if I was out of the way though, surely?"

"Oh I don't know." Frances looked out into the evening as they rode up the hill.

"Will you ask her to come and stay?"

"Do you want me to? I have Sarah."

"I know, but the question is, do you want to ask your mother?" he asked. She thought for a moment. "You did say you didn't want to be alone—even though Sarah lives with us—and I can't stand the thought of you feeling alone so... Beatrice will have to do."

"You don't mind?"

"What leg do I have to stand on? I'm that bastard leaving you again." He smiled.

"She understands. She does."

Frances recalled the last time he left her. She cried for weeks: while her infant slept beside her, while her infant suckled, while she rocked the baby's bassinet through the night, she cried. She remembered the long nights and blurred days. Sarah had been the light in a dark, dark tunnel, sharing the burden of motherhood in the early months and eventually, becoming a much needed aid to the family. It was Sarah who had helped her remember to feed herself, wash herself and dress, but it was her husband that she had wanted by her side. The thought of him leaving again crushed her.

She had pored over his letters, rereading them until the next ones came. She loved him and longed for him but their separation hurt her deeply. She wasn't sure if she could cope with another repeat of his long absence.

"I'm doing this for us, darling. Nothing in the world matters more than my family."

She blinked back tears. "I know. I know," she heard herself saying. "I just hate the thought of you leaving me."

Frances rested her head on his shoulder, trying not to think of the screaming woman in the mirror.

He locked the front door behind them when they arrived home. Frances gathered her skirts and charged up the stairs immediately, leaving him to stand in the hallway, accompanied only by the ticking of the grandfather clock and soon after, the closure of the bedroom door. He poured himself a brandy in the parlour room and waited, not knowing if it was safe to go to his own bed or not. Her mood had confused him.

As he had hoped, she returned, this time in what he had first thought was a white nightgown. "I wanted to get out of that thing."

"Must have been uncomfortable—wait—"

She sighed. "I can't get it off by myself."

He placed his drink down on the side table and walked over to her, placing his fingers on the outline of the corset that she was still wearing. "Then let me." They both knew that she could have called Maggie to come up and remove it, but it was obvious to him that Frances didn't want to. He gently loosened each crossed cord and untied the knots. "I don't know why women bother with these things," he grumbled.

She felt his face close to hers and whispered, "me neither." He lowered his hand down the front of her shift, feeling her nipples harden. "Maybe because we're all fools."

Within minutes, he was making love to her on the sofa of the parlour room. She moaned softly, looking over his head at the open door. At any moment, someone could walk in; the very thought of it drove her wild with lust, and she thrust her face into his neck to conceal her cry of pleasure when it overwhelmed her. She climbed onto his lap and groaned before collapsing into his chest, feeling him tense up and tremble inside her. He pulled her close to him, pushing a soft, relaxed breath into her ear.

The clock struck twelve, unlocking their lovestruck tangle and deafening them both into alertness. Frances, suddenly aware of her breast hanging out of her shift, covered up and rubbed her arms. Her skin was goose pimpled and stinging from the cold air. John reached for his jacket, pulled out his pocket watch and checked it. "This time it's right. Makes a nice change."

"Is it just me or is it quite cold in here?" she asked, watching clouds of icy breath leave her mouth. John seemed unperturbed at first as he rose from the sofa and pulled his trousers back on. They both heard the chiming of the clock slow down. She watched him suddenly stop what he was doing. The temperature in the room had fallen dramatically, and he felt it too.

"It's baltic in here," he said, as wisps of hot breath floated into the icy room before him. The air became thick, smothering them into silence as they looked at one another. Frances clenched her chattering teeth. With her gaze fixed on her husband, she saw the shadow pass through the hallway only in the corner of her eye. Unable to turn her head to look, she could only assume that it passed in the direction of the stairs, rendering her powerless to do anything but observe the rising terror in her throat. John's eyes didn't leave her face.

From the staircase, they heard the sound of something heavy being dragged along the tiles and onto the first carpeted step. It slid and gently thumped, sliding again, with another thump, and another, until the hallway finally fell silent. Frances swallowed and dared to turn her head. She saw nothing but the clock standing sentry in the hallway, its pendulum moving at a natural rhythm once more. She turned to look back at John to find an expression she had never seen cross his face until now: fear.

After a quick shot of brandy, John gingerly approached the staircase, looking up into the dimly-lit landing. Frances crept closely behind him, shivering within the shield of his body. She wanted nothing more than to get back to the bedroom and lie down in his arms, where it was safe.

They reached the top of the stairs where their bedroom was waiting for them, lit and arranged as though they had been there all night. Frances almost fell into the wall when she saw the red satin gown draped across the bed.

"That isn't where I left it."

"What?" he whispered.

"Th-th-the dress. I put it in the wardrobe."

John, having stuffed the dress into a chest in the guest room at Frances' insistence, went upstairs to check on Elsie and Sarah. Both were fast asleep. He returned to Frances soon after, reassuring her that everybody was fine. He assured her that he'd seen nothing but his reflection holding a candle in the mirrors that he passed. "Sometimes, when you're exhausted, you shiver a lot," he said softly, rubbing his hands up her bare arms to warm her. "It's not cold in here."

"I know what I saw," she said, folding them across her chest.

He let out a long sigh. "I've seen nothing in the house since. We're probably just tired."

They didn't talk any more about what they'd seen together. John, after lying in the bed in silence, eventually drifted off.

Frances, after some time, fell into a deep sleep, finding herself back at the hotel restaurant, sitting across the table from John, who had a moustache again.

"Do you think I enjoy it, Frances?" His tone had transformed from calm and apologetic to curt. "Do you think I like travelling across the world just to keep a wife?" His voice sounded like a low, pressurised hiss threatening to burst from his mouth. She saw his countenance darken, highlighting wolfish features on his thin face. "I have to work until I drop dead to keep my family. The least you could do is thank me for it. I've done nothing but work hard for you. Christ, I even sent flowers to your mother when your father died. I have yet to receive a thank you for taking care of everything."

She stared at him in shock. She had never seen him in this light. "I'm sorry," she whispered. "I didn't know—"

"Why would she have told you?" he snapped. "If she did, you'd think she had no good reason to despise me and she can't have that." He took a long sip of his wine and looked away in annoyance.

"It must be so hard for you, darling." She fought back tears. His face relaxed again and he broke the tension with a smile.

"I'd do anything for you."

"I know."

"Anyway, let's not think about it. I have to sign some papers and do a bit of business. That'll be it for a long time, possibly even forever. I'll be back home with you and Elsie after Christmas."

"That's not what you said yester—"

"What?" The music was louder now. His attention had drifted elsewhere.

As though she had awoken from a trance and watched from another table, she saw his eyes wander, fixing themselves on several glamorous women who passed them. "Oh yes, *before Christmas*, I meant," he said over his shoulder as one of the women smiled at him. Frances' sadness turned to unchecked, unrelenting, all-consuming jealousy. She wanted to get up and scream at them, telling them to leave him alone. He noticed her stare and returned to his meal. She watched him cut through the rare, bloody steak on his plate, tearing and chewing it vigorously. Its pink juices slipped from the corners of his mouth before he could dab them away with his napkin.

"You're not eating, darling," he said with a concerned glance. She looked down at her dish of blood, watching it grow colder by the minute. The woman in red was standing over their table, bent forward, heavy droplets of blood crashing down from her throat onto Frances' plate. Frances wiped the gentle spritz of splatter from her cheeks and looked up at John's disappointed face. "Mary made this just for you, and you're being rude."

The clock in the foyer of the hotel struck with a resounding bong, sending vibrations through her body, rattling her teeth. It struck again, forcing her onto her feet. "I want to go home," she declared.

John, as though immune to the clock's obnoxious striking, looked up at her in confusion. "What?"

"I want to go home. Now!"

12

THE VERY NEXT MORNING, Frances busied herself with emptying the wardrobe of the clothes she didn't want, and set to work altering the less extravagant items that she did want to keep. Mrs Mckinnon, as instructed, arranged for the gowns to be sold to a dressmaker on the high street, and left a copy of the dressmaker's brochure on the coffee table. Frances gasped at the prices and refused to order anything, much to her husband's disappointment.

"It'll take you months to make your own, Fan. Do you not even want *one*?" He had had his eye on a drawing of a beautiful satin gown with a deep v cut at the front and the back. Frances had liked it too, but wouldn't agree to order it.

"I will be able to make my own, just you watch," she said.

He clicked his tongue and sighed, "I'll make the next dinner reservation when hell freezes over, then."

She slammed her sewing down on her lap. "What else do you think I'll be doing for the next three months? You won't be here and I'll have nothing else to do. I can do it, John." She surprised herself at the irritation in her voice and softened. "Please, I want to do this. I've asked Mrs Mckinnon to fetch me some more fabric from the market. There was something about those dresses... they were—"

"Haunted?" He smirked and widened his eyes comically. "I suppose the house could be haunted," he began. "Perhaps you were possessed last night. Haven't seen you like *that* before."

She reddened and resumed her sewing. "You laugh but... my mother thinks the house is haunted."

"You're joking?" he rolled his eyes.

"John, deny it all you want but you saw something last night. It wasn't just me."

"I saw nothing. It was a shadow, if that. Could have been anything. You know I don't believe in all that, anyway."

"You were afraid," she said quietly. He bristled as her eyes met his.

"Everything was fine, woman. We're not sitting here mithering over nothing."

She wasn't listening. "That's three of us, now. My mother—"

"It's just nit-picking'!" He ran his fingers through his hair in exasperation. "There was always going to be something wrong with it, seen as it belongs to me, eh?" he said with a shrug. "That good for nothing you married can't even pick a decent house." Putting his hands in his pockets, he looked at her again. "That woman has aged me, Frances. Not Australia and the hard graft—that woman." He pointed to the wall, which Frances had surmised must have been in the direction of West Derby. "I need to just get used to it. That's my life but dear God, can she not just wind it in? I don't need her turning this house into the next sensation." His wife had remained bent over her work, with a tightened face. Knowing better than to continue with his rant, he sighed. "All right, you want to talk about it some more. You're not joking?"

"No," she shook her head fervently, lifting her eyes to look at him again. "She not only informed me that she believes this house to be haunted but..." she shook her head and shrugged, "she told me that the postman is a medium. You remember Mr Kingsley? The postman?"

The thought of Trevor Kingsley conducting seances and speaking to the dead immediately disarmed John. "Ha!" He shook his head in disbelief. "Not Mr Kingsley?"

"The very same. Apparently he helps people rid their homes of ghosts."

He rolled his eyes. "I see."

Frances placed the chemise she was working on on her lap and dropped her shoulders. "It's going to be interesting having her around for a couple of months. You're getting a lucky escape." A faint flicker of amusement lifted the corners of her mouth.

"I'm sure you'll have a ball," he said, opening his newspaper. "I'll be so sorry to have missed it."

Later that afternoon, Elsie was sitting on her father's bouncing knee as he sang half-remembered nursery rhymes to her. Frances smiled and shook her head every time he misremembered a word or a name.

"Daddy, it's not that," Elsie said.

"Isn't it? I thought you go to Charing Cross to see a white baby upon a white horse?"

"Lady, Daddy. Lay-dee!"

"Oh yes that's it. With rings on her fingers and bells on her toes..."

"She will have music, wherever she goes!" Elsie added with a proud smile. "Daddy?"

"Yes?"

"What's Charing Cross?"

"It's the middle of London."

"Oh." Elsie's mouth turned downward.

"What did you think it was?"

"A burnt bun."

Realising that she meant *a hot cross bun*. Frances and John locked eyes and erupted with laughter. "That's charring, darling. Bless your heart." John lifted her and placed her on the floor, handing her one of her dolls.

Frances shook her head and said, "it's Banbury Cross."

John paused for a moment, lifting his eyes to the ceiling while he sang the song in his head. He laughed and returned his gaze to Frances. "So it is!" he said. "Elsie, you trickster." He chased after her and tickled her when he caught her. Her laughter filled the room like bubbles overflowing from a cup. When the little girl had had enough and begged him to stop, he let go and walked over to the door, straightening his jacket.

"Are you off out?" asked Frances.

"Yes. I need some more cigars."

"You've run out already?"

He nodded gravely. He wouldn't say as much, but Frances felt he hadn't been the same since the incident in the hallway. Something troubled him. It troubled them both. When she'd told him of her dream, he laughed and said, "I'd never speak to you like that, you madwoman." She thought that maybe she was a madwoman, and should keep her thoughts to herself. Who would believe her if she said the red dress had somehow managed to take itself out of the wardrobe and languish on the bed? She shuddered at the thought, trying to maintain focus on her work. The sewing helped, but it didn't block her unwanted thoughts completely.

"You'd better go and get some then," she said, pulling some ivory thread through the eye of her needle.

"I won't be long." He bent down and kissed Elsie on the head and crossed the room to do the same to his wife. Her eyes followed him until he left the room, passing Sarah, who came into the drawing room to find Elsie. "Elsie, it's time to tidy the nursery, young lady. Those dollies have been running amok up there."

"That wasn't me," Elsie said, stroking Blissy's hair.

"Elsie, don't tell lies," her mother added sternly. "There are no lies in this house. Now go and do as Sarah says."

"It wasn't me, Mummy," she said again, turning her gaze to Frances. "It was Mary. She's upset."

Frances, distracted by the mention of Mary's name, stabbed herself in the thumb with her needle. She brought it away from the cream fabric and into her mouth. "Go and do it, Elsie!" she snapped, stemming the blood from the pricked thumb with her tongue.

Elsie flinched and looked down at the floor.

"Come on, Elsie. Do as your mother says," Sarah folded her arms and waited until Elsie left the room, dragging her feet as she did so. Sarah followed, leaving Frances to work in silence.

According to the drawing room window, the weather outside was damp and grey, lining the windows with a fine drizzle. Frances turned in her seat to try and get more light on her work, but as she turned her head away, she thought she'd caught a glimpse of someone entering the room. She turned her head sharply to look behind her and saw nothing. The sideboard on the wall behind her was as it had always been. There was nobody there. "You're imagining things," she muttered to herself.

After half an hour of failing to effectively sew a straight line, Frances placed her sewing back in the basket beside the chair and walked out into the hallway, pacing up and down the black and white tiles with her hands on her hips. She stopped dead in her tracks when she saw the outline of John in the painted glass around the front door. "What is he doing?" she whispered to herself. He had his back turned to her, and from what she could make out, he wasn't wearing his hat or his jacket. She walked towards the door and wrestled with the surprisingly stiff handle to let him in. The door was locked. "I just need to unlock it," she said, bringing her face close to the glass. He didn't move. Frances turned and rummaged through the drawer of the side table for the key. When she checked over her shoulder to see if he was still there, she saw him slowly moving away. "John, it's locked!" she called. "Where's your key?" His silhouette grew smaller as she picked up the right key and inserted it into the lock. By the time she had opened the door, the doorstep was empty. She looked out left and right of the garden path. "What in the—?" She stepped down into the front garden and looked around again, trying the side gate. It was also locked.

"Good afternoon, ma'am," Mrs Mckinnon called as she approached the front gate. "I have your fabrics!" She proudly lifted up a generously sized bundle. "They had everything you asked for."

"Mrs Mckinnon, was my husband here?"

She looked around at the street, and said, "no, ma'am. Are you expecting him?"

Frances shook her head, bewildered. "No. I thought he was—" she turned and pointed to the open front door. "Never mind."

Mrs Mckinnon followed her into the house and closed the door. "Where do you want me to keep the fabrics, ma'am?"

"The sideboard in there, please."

Mrs Mckinnon bustled into the drawing room with her bundle. "It's a bit dreich out there, ma'am. Would you like a cup of tea when I've folded these away?"

Frances, not listening, looked at the glass around the door one more time. She wondered if she was losing her mind after all.

13

JOHN HAD BEEN GONE no more than a week by the time Frances had had enough of her mother's company. In moments of desperation, she had hidden herself away writing furiously to John, expressing her thoughts, regrets and sharing the happiest memories she had with him. He had left an address for her to write but she felt she still had more to say, so they remained folded and in the drawer of her writing desk. When she returned to them to see if anything should be added, she tore them up after deciding nothing she had written was worthy of a letter.

He had kissed her farewell on the doorstep and climbed into the cab, waving goodbye to everyone before they watched his transport fade like a speck of soot, blending into the greying distance. Frances waved with red, swollen eyes and cried for the rest of the morning in private until Beatrice forced her to straighten herself up and play a game of rummy.

"You need to eat, you know," Beatrice said at dinner. Frances pushed some food around her plate.

"I'm not hungry."

"You think you're not, but you must be. You'll be no good to us starved."

Frances reluctantly brought some food to her lips. The potato tasted like chalk, but she ate it anyway, gulping down some water to push it along.

The milk pudding they had for dessert was more palatable. Mrs Mckinnon cleared the dinner plates away as though they were empty. Frances felt as though she'd been a rude house guest in someone else's home; she watched the old woman take them away politely with her kind smile and endeavoured to try harder with the pudding.

"I was wondering if you wanted to do that seance," Beatrice said, dropping a dollop of jam into her bowl.

"Seance?"

"Yes, you know, with Mr Kingsley?"

"I didn't say I wanted to have a seance."

"No, I know, but you did agree that the house was haunted."

"I don't know why I said that."

"Are you sure? Elsie says it's haunted."

"Have you asked her that?"

"No. It's just the things she says."

Frances, about to roll her eyes, stopped herself and looked at the floor instead. "What does she say?"

Beatrice cleared her throat and with a lowered voice, said, "says she sees a man in the house sometimes. Mary says he's a bad man and that we should stay away from him."

Frances scoffed and shook her head. "What nonsense."

"It's not," Beatrice said sternly. "She's seen him in her room. He watches Sarah sleeping."

Frances felt her stomach churning. "What?" she asked, dropping her spoon.

Beatrice's guests arrived the following afternoon. After Maggie had taken their hats and coats and led them into the drawing room, Beatrice introduced Mr Kingsley and his son-in-law, Fred Wilcox to Frances. Mr Kingsley was around the same age as Beatrice, with a grey, broom-like moustache, a balding head and long lashes on his smiling eyes. Frances couldn't help but like the old man. He was kind, polite and welcoming, with a deep voice. Fred, in contrast, was a much shorter man, with a severe, square jaw and a wide face that was only exacerbated by his ginger mutton chops.

"How nice to meet you," Fred said, offering a hand to Frances. "I am Mr Kingsley's assistant."

"Fred is my daughter's husband. He's also my solicitor."

"Handy," said Frances, with a welcoming smile.

"Indeed. It was lucky we could come tonight. My daughter—Florence—she's the organist at church and it's her evening to practise. I'm sure Fred is happy to be here instead of on his own all evening."

"Indubitably," Fred agreed. "I'm not much of a musician, nor do I have an ear for music apart from the odd sing-song—No offence," he said, looking at his father-in-law, who waved a hand.

"None taken. We can't all have the gift, can we?" Mr Kingsley said with a straight face. "Now tell me, Mrs Bryant, have you ever been to, or hosted a seance before?" His tone was gentle and soothing, like that of a family doctor or a priest. He spoke to Frances as though calming a cat with a bristled tail out of a corner.

"No," she said as she shook her head lightly. "I'll be honest, Mr Kingsley, I never thought I'd need to."

"Please, call me Trevor," he said in his deep, Lancashire drawl. "This is a type of meeting, shall we say? A seance is a meeting where we, for whatever reason, attempt to contact the dead. It'll take us into a place that sits between the land of the living and the land of the dead."

"Like purgatory?" Frances asked, earning a suspicious look from her mother. "I know that's what the Catholics call it, is all—you know—a waiting place?"

"Sort of, I suppose." He nodded. "I'd say that's a good way to describe it, cocker." He arranged some items on the table: some slate, a stick of chalk, a ouija board and some candles. "I see you already have some candles but, these are just in case."

"Just in case of what?" asked Frances, nosing over the items.

"In case we run out. Sometimes, the flames can intensify. It's only ghosts saying 'ow do?' but it's a bit much for us sometimes. They leave us in the dark."

"Quite literally," Beatrice snorted. Frances looked up at her in horror.

"You've done this before?" she asked her mother.

Beatrice nodded sheepishly. "I've been to a few, yes."

Frances, seeing her mother in a new light, sat with her mouth agape. Mr Kingsley, oblivious to the silent stand off, continued with his briefing. "I can't tell you how it's going to go tonight simply because these spirits are unpredictable. Sometimes they're queuing up and others, well, we'll just be sat here. I need to know that you're all right with that, Mrs Bryant," he said, looking up at her from the table. Frances twiddled her fingers.

"I'm not sure I have any other choice, Mr—Trevor, sorry. My mother is convinced there's something in the house with us and to be perfectly honest, I think I am, also."

Trevor Kingsley leaned back in the chair, seeming pleased with Frances' answer. "Very well," the old man said as Fred brought more chairs to the card table they were sitting at. "Now, can you tell me who's taking part and who's in the house?"

"Myself and my mother are joining you and Fred. Elsie, my daughter, she will be in bed. Sarah, her nanny, will be in the house but I don't think she wants to join in with this. Other than that, there's Mrs Mckinnon, my housekeeper and Maggie, my maid. They'll be in their quarters, I imagine."

"Is there a chance I could speak to Sarah and the little'un before we do the seance? It helps paint a picture, so to speak."

Frances agreed. "They will have dinner with us. We can speak then."

At dinner, Elsie was cherubic in her demeanour and, knowing that sitting at the dinner table was a rare treat, made a keen effort to charm the company. The affable Trevor Kingsley was taken with the little girl as she told him all about her dolls and her favourite games. Frances, although prepared for the conversation, felt herself overcome with nausea every time Mary was mentioned. Fred, observing her discomfort, poured her some water. "Children are masterful at creating imaginary friends, aren't they?" Fred said quietly as Elsie spoke to Trevor Kingsley.

"Oh yes, they are," she said, thanking him for the water. She sipped it nervously.

"I had an imaginary friend, when I was little," said Sarah. "Another little girl. I think her name was Rachel. Did you have one, ma'am?"

"No, no I didn't. At least, I don't remember one."

"Mine was a dog," Fred said, sipping his wine. "My mother wouldn't let me have one of my own, so I made one up."

Frances and Sarah laughed at Fred's confession. "His name was Barney," he said wistfully, resting his chin on his hand.

"What happened to him?" asked Frances.

Fred shook his head, "I don't very much know. I think I simply grew up."

"Perhaps it was a ghost," Beatrice said, slicing some cheese. "We could be seeing them all the time, for all we know."

"Indeed," he agreed. "Though I should think the spirits of animals are unlikely."

Beatrice turned her face toward Fred and frowned. "Why would you say that?" she asked in a lowered voice, raising an eyebrow. "I've heard of plenty of ghost stories concerning farmhouses and manors where packs of dogs can be heard howling in the night, leaving their muddy paw prints everywhere, all while the living ones are asleep at the foot of their masters' beds."

Frances shuddered. "Don't say that, mother. You know I'll have trouble sleeping."

"Trouble sleeping about what?" enquired Trevor Kingsley over his shoulder.

"Nothing," Fred said. "Nothing that the little one should be in earshot of, anyway."

After seeing Elsie to bed and giving her a goodnight kiss, Frances entered the landing and closed the nursery door behind her. Sarah didn't know what Beatrice had said about the sightings in her room, and it seemed Elsie hadn't told her either. Frances sighed with relief but a knot of fear still sat within her core, squeezing her insides as she breathed. "It's bloody well nothing, Frances," she tried to tell herself, hearing John's voice in her head. *I'm a madwoman. What the hell are we doing? I shall write him and mention this bizarre evening. I'm sure he'll find it entertaining, if nothing else.*

She giddily descended the staircase, taking no notice of the flickering sconces as she passed them. She arrived in the tiled hallway to see that everybody else had gone into the drawing room. Leaning closer to the door, Frances could hear the clinking of glasses and rolled her eyes: Beatrice was entertaining.

She opened the door and found the room almost unrecognisable with the closed curtains and tablecloth that Mr Kingsley had brought. "Ready when you are, cocker," he said with a wink. He gestured to one of the still empty chairs. "Mind the candles."

There were what seemed like hundreds of them, glowing with a fierce, yellow haze around the room.

Beatrice was the last to be seated, having lit the final candle for the seance. "There," she said, proudly. "All ready for you now, Trevor."

Mr Kingsley nodded and cleared his throat. "Everyone here wants to take part, yes?" he asked.

Sarah, although intrigued by the prospect of a seance, had bowed out earlier and remained upstairs with Elsie. "Probably for the best. I wouldn't want to know about being watched in my sleep either," Beatrice had said. "Best she doesn't know anything."

"We're all here, Mr K—Trevor," said Frances, wincing. The room, darkened by the closure of dense curtains and glaring candlelight, felt heavy with anticipation. Frances sensed her heart beating violently as she looked around the room. The candles, at first glowing and fierce, had reduced to a subdued flicker, as though there was a draught that had narrowly missed the blockade of curtains.

"Very well. Now, everybody needs to hold on to the glass here." Mr Kingsley pointed to the tumbler that Frances had assumed was for Beatrice's happy hour and smirked. "Don't let go of the glass, even if it moves. The glass will be moving around to these letters here." Everyone looked across the board at the letters as Mr Kingsley set the tumbler face down. Frances took a deep breath. She didn't want to know who Mary was, or the other man. She wanted everyone and everything to go away, but instead, she placed her finger on the glass. Fred, Beatrice and Mr Kingsley followed.

"If there is anyone present tonight, please tell us," commanded Mr Kingsley in a booming, clear voice. Frances, deafened by the sound of her own breath, waited with the group in silence, staring at the tumbler. Hours seemed to pass by as they waited. "If Mary is here. Please give us a sign."

Frances felt the tug of the glass before she saw it. Their hands were carefully guided to the Y, the E and the S. "Yes. Mary is here," Mr Kingsley said, half to the room and half to himself. He looked at Frances and gave a gentle, encouraging nod.

"Did you die here, Mary?" Frances flushed red at hearing her own question. *Of course she bloody died.* "I mean..." her mind emptied within seconds as her eyes met those of another woman across the table. Sitting between Fred and Beatrice was the woman she had seen in the mirror. Beatrice inhaled a sharp breath as the glass dragged across the letters Y, E and S again.

Frances allowed the glass to move her hand but she could not take her eyes off the pallid face belonging to the figure sitting opposite her. "Mary," she tried to say, locking the apparition in her gaze. "M-m," she tried again. She thought of the throat, the blood and the scream as the others waited in silence for something else to happen. They couldn't see the ghost in the room.

"Frances, what is it?" Beatrice asked with a furrowed brow. "Frances? Frances? Speak to me!"

Mary's eyes, darkened around the lids, were wide and frightened. She opened her mouth and screamed.

Before Frances could blink, she felt the tumbler rumbling under her finger, vibrating with tension until it shattered. Beatrice yelped and covered her face as the tiny pieces of the tumbler scattered across the table. When she looked up, Frances was still staring at a space beside her, as though in a trance. She rushed over to her daughter and placed her hands on her shoulders. "Frances, what's wrong? Frances? Please speak to me! Trevor! What do I do?" She gave Frances another shake. "What do I do?"

"Leave her, Beatrice. She'll come to in a moment." Mr Kingsley slowly removed Beatrice from her daughter and stood back. "Mary, can you hear us?" he asked, looking about the room.

To Beatrice's relief, Frances closed her eyes and took a deep breath. "She's here in the room with us," she said.

Part II

14

Autumn in the city had been wet, laden with fog and a still, damp chill that settled in the bone by evening. From the tall red chimneys of the factories, the smoke rose, poisoning mother nature's sweet breath and staining it with hues of yellow, grey and black. Down on the river, horns blasted as ships rolled in, waiting impatiently for the dockers to unload. The air was thick with the scent of tobacco and burning coal, sinking into the street with a dense, ominous smog. Hordes of dockers and ragged children shuffled down toward the factories and warehouses, barely looking up as they walked.

Further up the hill, amidst the bustle of bankers and traders heading to their respective places of work, a small urchin weaved his way through overcoats, shoes and trams, missing some of them by a hair. Like a shadow, the boy was gone within a blink, appearing again on the far side of the perilous cobbled street. Some days, he'd stay closer to the crowds and see what he could find in their pockets, but today he was on a mission. Dodging horse droppings, cigarette butts and the trample of boots, eight-year-old Paulie McRae could have impersonated a phantom, he was so swift. No informant had ever been so masterful at such a young age.

Waiting for the boy on a quiet corner of the street was Inspector Daniel Muldoon, his breath rising before him in wisps of white cloud. He chewed his tobacco pensively, watching for the boy to reappear. His hands were firmly settled in his pockets as he looked out at the rows of sad, brick buildings that occupied his line of sight. When the boy had successfully crossed the street, Muldoon greeted him with a solemn nod. "You ought to get yourself some new shoes, Paulie," he said, looking down at the boy's filthy, bare feet on the pavement.

"Last time I had shoes, me da beat me. He says he needs all me slummy." The boy handed him a scrap of paper. Muldoon eyed him up and down and noticed the threadbare shirt, torn trousers that he'd long outgrown and shuddered. Winter would be cold.

Muldoon took the note from the boy and began to open it. "What's he needing the money for?" he asked, with a raised eyebrow.

The boy shrugged. Muldoon turned his head and spat the tobacco out onto the damp pavement. *Drink, no doubt*, he thought, but he said nothing and instead read the note. The boy watched the detective's face with a keen anticipation, as though he was going to read it out to the illiterate child in the manner of a bedtime story.

"Thanks, Paulie. Now get yourself some shoes and don't wear them where your da can see, you hear me?" He tossed a shilling to the boy, who jumped up and caught it gratefully like a circus monkey.

"Thanks Dooney," he said, smiling with scattered teeth that seemed too large for his head. *Dooney*. They were friends now. Muldoon watched him skip off and disappear within the throng of passers-by before he turned away and began to stroll up to Cheapside.

Standing out on the hill like a warning to all would-be-miscreants was The Main Bridewell. Muldoon felt that the small, slit windows watched like narrowed eyes in the face of an unsmiling, hostile guardsman. Inside, the corridors of the main bridewell were gloomy and seemingly endless, but luckily for Muldoon, he never had to visit more than one room in the building.

Waiting for him in the Police Chief Inspector's office was his unofficial employer, Andrew Gill. Gill had just finished speaking to a young constable in a manner Muldoon and many others recognised as 'the skinning'. Whoever this lad was, he'd made a fool of himself and Muldoon guessed he had caught the tail end of the reckoning on his way down. Knowing better than to be caught eavesdropping on Gill, he stood back from the door as he heard heavy footsteps approaching. It swung open with a loud shriek and out came a gangly young man in uniform, no older than twenty. His face still held some childlike roundness, but his cheeks were flushed crimson as though Gill had given each one a hard slap. The constable in question, upon seeing Muldoon in the corridor, concealed his embarrassment with a sneer and muttered "mick" under his breath as he passed.

"Now now, son," Muldoon said quietly. "We all have a little Irish in us. Just ask your ma."

The young man, predictably cocky and hot-blooded, leapt into Muldoon's trap like a bated bear. Just as he was about to lunge at the grinning Irishman, Gill blocked him with his large, stout frame. "That's enough. Lacey," he growled, "now sling yer hook. You've got real work to do or you're out." He brought his face closer to that of the young constable's. "If I hear one more word–", he wagged a fat finger, "one more word! I'll be posting those big bollocks to your mother. Now get lost."

Constable Lacey, knowing that the purple-skinned glower of Andrew Gill was not to be challenged, lowered his head and slunk away down the echoey corridor. "Mulders, come in and close the door," Gill barked over his shoulder. Muldoon followed him into the large, almost-bare office where Gill gestured for him to sit down as he remained standing, lighting his pipe. He angrily puffed once or twice and pulled it away from his mouth.

"Young and stupid. Can't work with 'em, can't work without 'em. Good legs for catching robbers but God they're stupid." He blew out some smoke and furiously puffed again.

If Muldoon had ever wondered what a bulldog smoking a pipe looked like, he had to look no further than Chief Inspector

Gill across the desk for an accurate picture. He smirked. "I'm sorry I missed it."

Gill was calming down. Muldoon recognised the decrease in effort in Gill's smoke inhalation and the drawing out of the exhales. "Go on then," Gill sighed, "our cellar bodies?" Tobacco smoke seeped out of his nostrils as he waited for an answer.

"Human, sir."

"Christ," Gill said, looking up at the ceiling. "Just what we need." He shook his head and slapped a large hand down onto the desk. "Even the barrel of babies?"

Muldoon drew a deep breath. "Even the barrel of babies," he said regretfully. "I'm afraid the pickled bodies are the work of a..." he reached into his pocket for the scrap of paper again and opened it, "Glyn and Fisher," he said. "Both William. Should be easy. They drink in The Corner House on Scotland Road—all the time, actually. I'd be drinking too, mind. They've been sending the corpses to Edinburgh to a surgeon there, who's using an alias. But you'll love this—John Smith is his real name, would you believe? I'm sure a flying squad can sort it. The address is overleaf."

"Body snatching. Makes me sick," Gill hissed, scowling into oblivion.

"Easy work if you can get it. The workhouse doesn't check who's buying, they just want rid... these fellas are making a mint. Ten pounds a corpse, allegedly." He slid the note across the desk, where Gill grabbed it and inspected it with his head cocked to one side.

"You're sure? John Smith is a surgeon?"

"Yes."

"Damn. I was sure this one was one for you." Gill, in his twenty years of policing, had been noticeably horrified by the case. "Poor young Robertson found them. I tried to console him with the old 'a man couldn't have done this,' talk. Turns out I'm wrong. I'm bloody wrong. Christ."

"Aye, well, sometimes man surprises you." Muldoon shrugged and looked about the room at the peeling wallpaper and rotting wood frames of the tall, filthy office windows and wondered how much longer he'd have to stay in the miserable bridewell. Every time he came in, he felt he'd entered a maze. He hated it. In the courtyard downstairs, he could hear the iron doors unbolting as prisoners were sent out for daily exercise. A football slammed against an outside wall, rattling the thinly paned window, shocking his consciousness back into the room where Gill was marching to the window swinging his arms in fury. "I told ye no fucking balls!" he bellowed into the courtyard with a slight waver that only Muldoon could hear. His order was immediately followed by the blow of a whistle and the faint arguing between some male voices below. "Those do-gooders say they need exercise. I say fuck off and let me do my job," he said, still at the window. Muldoon said nothing and sat back, watching.

Judging by the way he hung his head on the way back to his seat, Gill seemed devastated. "All right, but God it's a bad one. You can see why I thought...?" He drew some more smoke from his pipe and blew a plume of grey clouds into the room via his nostrils and waved a hand dismissively. "Well there's something else that might interest you anyway. I don't think it's one for us." He rested the pipe in the corner of his mouth and leaned over the desk, his large body towering over Muldoon. "Do you have many dealings with ghosts, Mulders?"

"Not really," he shrugged. "They're usually harmless. Who's ever been killed by a ghost?" He shrugged again with a half laugh. "Demons, sure, I'll take a look. Ghosts, though?"

Gill was less than impressed with Muldoon's dismissive tone. A deeply superstitious man, Andrew Gill did not enjoy ghost stories, nor did he partake in making light of them. He tried again. "What about possessions? Exorcisms, that kind of thing?"

"I'm no priest, sir. Anyway, I didn't think you'd be needing my services much longer."

"Why's that?"

"I told you, I don't deal with general crime. You know that, Gov." He wasn't sure why he called Gill, *Gov*. It was just what they were used to. "And I'm no priest."

"No," Gill felt himself becoming annoyed with his slippery contractor, "but you are a Catholic and your kind deal with… all *that*."

"All that?"

"Yes, Mulders. Weird shit. You deal with weird shit, and there's been a lot of it knocking around. I can't afford to let you go just yet."

Daniel Muldoon, lead detective: weird shit, he thought, looking up at Gill who was still thinking.

"Look," he said, sitting down in his seat, finally. "This is a sensitive case I've got. I've had a woman here, a Mrs Mckinnon. She says she's concerned for the welfare of her mistress, who hasn't been the same since they had a little seance and the bloody thing went tits up."

Muldoon crossed his legs. "Is that so?"

Gill opened a drawer and pulled out a case file. He slid it across the desk to Muldoon who reluctantly opened it. Inside was a family photograph. His eye was drawn first to the fair-haired beauty standing beside a taller, dark-haired man. In front of them was a little girl, looking up at the lens with large, clear eyes. "Just showing you the woman because she doesn't look like that at the moment."

"What happened to her?"

"That's for you to find out. Mrs Mckinnon brought these in with her statement. The men at the desk weren't very kind to the old lady, naturally, what with her saying her mistress is possessed and all, but she knows *my* housekeeper and managed to get it all to me. I don't deal in the supernatural, but you do. I promised I'd send someone."

Muldoon leaned back with a furrowed brow, closing the file. "This all seems a bit... domestic, don't you think?"

Gill said nothing. He puffed on his pipe, glaring at the Irishman. Muldoon sighed. "Where's this woman then?" he asked, realising this was not optional.

Gill smiled. "Percy street. Number five. I get the impression that the sooner you go, the better, to be honest. Try and speak to her doctor as well. Her name is Frances Bryant, but you'll be dealing with Mrs Mckinnon."

"You don't think she's just ill? Hysteria? There's always room in—"

"No. No I don't," he said gravely, leaning forward. "From what I've been told," he said in a quiet voice, "it's one for you."

15

MULDOON RANG THE BELL and waited. Turning to look out at the street, it was picturesque, like the illustrations he'd seen on postcards in the post office; it felt a far cry from the slums and high streets he frequented. He pulled his collar closer to his neck, as though disguising himself from potential onlookers. Deciduous trees along the street were thinning out, wearing laced crowns of red, gold and green. The air, still with a lingering mist, felt warmer in the mid-morning sun as it glistened on the wet pavement before him. The sound of a click and a creak snapped him out of his observation.

At the door was a small, thin young maid with a sickly pallor. She looked up at his dark, towering figure and said nothing. Realising that he would have to speak instead, Muldoon cleared his throat and introduced himself. "I'm Inspector Muldoon. Here to see Mrs McKinnon, if I may." He flashed a small card.

The maid barely looked at it, nodded and opened the door wider. "Th-the kitchen, sir." She looked down at the floor with long, pale eyelashes and waited for him to step through, which he did—quietly. The house was still. He looked around, taking stock of the beautiful grandfather clock in the hallway, stuck on the incorrect time but still ticking. *Where's the wake?* he thought, absorbing the bleakness of the house: even the parlour palm beside the staircase looked sad. The maid said nothing and continued to look at the floor as he removed his hat and held it in his hands. "I'll show you the way," she said, closing the door silently with a click.

Muldoon, impressed by the grandeur of the tiled hallway overall, wiped his feet slightly on the mat and followed the black and white waif toward the back kitchen. As he passed the stairwell, something in the corner of his eye flickered. He turned to see a door of one of the rooms slightly open. Behind the door peeked a little blonde head that disappeared almost as quickly as it came before someone hurried over with a loud shush and firmly closed it. Immediately after, the faint tinkling on a piano emanated from the newly closed-off room. He smirked again: music lessons.

He turned his attention back to the maid and followed her down a dark passage to the open-doored kitchen, where a small, grey-haired lady was hard at work kneading bread on the table. She stopped as soon as Maggie entered and waited, smiling encouragingly.

"In-In-Inspector..." Maggie stuttered before letting out a deep breath, "Muldoon."

Violet Mckinnon looked up at the tall man behind her, smiled and nodded, as though pleased to have had a conversation with a small child. "Thank you, Maggie," she said. "I'll take it from here." Registering the polite dismissal, the girl spun around as fast as she could and scurried out of the room.

"Rather a jumpy one," Muldoon remarked, standing at the far end of the room. He found a brass hook on the wall and placed his hat on it, returning his hands to his deep, black pockets. Mrs Mckinnon fiercely wiped her hands on her white apron and marched over to the inspector, offering him her hand.

"I'm Violet Mckinnon, Inspector. Thank you for coming." Her handshake was firm. Assured.

He released a hand from one of his pockets and shook hers. Puffs of white flour rose into the air as he let go. "I'm sorry," she chuckled, "I was baking bread. Let me put the kettle on and we can speak some more. Would you like tea or coffee?"

"Coffee please. Black."

He watched the old lady busy herself with cups and crockery. "It needs to prove anyway," she said, layering a cloth over the bowl where the dough sat balled and waiting. "I'll just sort this out and I'll be right with you." She arranged the kitchen with a grace he'd never seen before, and seemed happy in her work. "Please sit down, Inspector... Muldoon, wasn't it?" she asked as she placed the kettle on the stove and lit the flame.

"Aye," he said, removing his heavy woollen jacket and placing it on the back of the chair. He pulled it out and sat down. "Chief Inspector Gill sent me, as you probably know."

She rested her hands on the sink and looked out of the kitchen window for a moment, turning her face slightly to talk, "I didn't know if anyone would come," she said in a quiet voice. He could sense the relief in her words as she spoke. "It's been... it's been weeks. The doctor can't help—he just gives her... *medicine* or so he calls it. The medium can't help. Mrs Larkin—that's my mistress' mother—is beside herself. It's a right ungodly mess." She turned to face him, finally. "Mrs Bryant..." she shook her head, "she didn't even want to do a seance, you know? Her mother suggested it." Her eyes were twinkling with the emerging dew of emotion as she wrung her hands on her apron again.

"Why was that?"

"Frances—Mrs Bryant—she said she could see something in the house. Well, rather, *feel* something but her mother convinced her to..." Violet Mckinnon looked toward the door and having decided that no one was there, returned her gaze to the detective, "you know, contact the dead?"

She had piqued Muldoon's interest with the mention of a seance. "What happened next?" he asked, leaning back in the chair.

Violet Mckinnon was just about to speak when they were interrupted by the shrill scream of the kettle. The housekeeper jumped out of her skin and laughed slightly, placing her hand on her chest. "Things have been so tense. I'm rather jumpy. Just let me get the coffee on and we'll talk some more, Inspector."

He watched the housekeeper pour boiling water into the coffee pot and seal it with the blue glazed lid. Coffee-scented steam sailed out of the spout and into the cool morning air of the room, invading his nostrils and sharpening his senses. She brought it to the table and laid out the matching blue cups and sugar bowl. "You said no milk, was that right?"

"Aye. No milk."

She nodded and sat down directly opposite. "They did the seance in the end. Poor Mrs Bryant hasn't been the same since. She says... she says she saw *Mary* at the table."

"This table?"

"No, the one in the drawing room. They had the seance in there and it was—I mean, I wasn't there but Mrs Larkin said it was awful. Mary, you see—Mary is this ghost they've been trying to contact. First the glass smashed everywhere and Mrs Bryant started talking nonsense... like she was possessed." Mrs Mckinnon poured the long ribbon of silky brown liquid into both cups and pushed one toward Muldoon, who took it gratefully. He admired her steady hand considering the topic of conversation. "I've never seen her so," Mrs Mckinnon seemed to look beyond him as she spoke, "so very different. Like she's not really here." Her lovely sharp eyes permeated through the crescent shaped spectacles on the end of her nose as she spoke to him. "She's not the same, Inspector."

"Who do you think is possessing Mrs Bryant?" Muldoon asked, sipping the coffee. It was fine coffee, and if it hadn't been made clear to him already, he was in a wealthy woman's house; she only drank the best. As though she could read him, the housekeeper said "Mrs Bryant is ever so kind. That's how I know something isn't right... but as for what or who is possessing her?"

Violet Mckinnon brought her eyes to inspect his face. Although like many men, a small area of his face bore the scars of smallpox, she thought he was handsome, if not in a gruff way. His ice-blue eyes cut through her like steel as she studied him. "I don't know," she said. "That's why I asked for help."

"Would it be possible for me to see Mrs Bryant?" he asked calmly.

For the first time since meeting Mrs Mckinnon, he could smell fear. Her pale eyes looked away, unsure where to go next. "You could... I suppose. I mean, you'll have to, eventually, will you not?" Muldoon felt heavy in the chair. Gill had been the same; he wasn't simply acting out of respect—he had been afraid when he said *it's one for you.* Violet Mckinnon's words had hit him with the same magnitude.

He nodded slowly. "I could interview the others first, if that's better?"

Violet Mckinnon brought her hand to her mouth and shook her head. "I don't know," she said.

"Perhaps I could explore the house first, then?"

"Of course. Could you wait here while I let Mrs Larkin know?"

"Yes." He sipped some more coffee. "I'll wait."

Violet Mckinnon returned to the kitchen a quarter of an hour later. "Mrs Larkin is with my mistress in the master bedroom. If you need to see the room, you'll have to give her fair warning. Mrs Bryant sleeps a lot, you see, and we don't want to disturb her."

"How much is fair warning?" he asked, raising one of his thick black eyebrows.

Mrs Mckinnon shook her head, "a day?"

Christ, he thought. "I'll take a look around the ground floor and the other rooms, but I'll have to come back to see Mrs Bryant's room tomorrow. Is that going to be all right with Mrs Larkin?"

The old lady thought for a moment. "Tell you what, I'll come with you when it's time to go to the first floor. I'll ask Mrs Larkin on my way up."

Muldoon began to roll his sleeves up. "Very well. May I begin in the basement?"

"Oh, that's mine and Maggie's quarters. Do you need to be going in there?"

"It's the whole house, Mrs Mckinnon..." he said, looking at her searchingly. She relented with a nod and a smile.

"Of course. I'm sorry—this is the first time—"

He raised a hand. "Say no more of it, Mrs Mckinnon. You're not the first to have found a paranormal investigation a little unsettling."

She seemed taken aback by his straightforwardness. "Is that what we're calling it? A paranormal investigation?"

"Well, you said it yourself, Mrs Mckinnon, in your letter, did you not? It's not one for the regular police." He stood up from the table and looked at her expectantly. "How do I get downstairs, then?"

16

ALTHOUGH HE HAD INSISTED that everybody act as normal while he conducted his inspection of the house, Muldoon felt he had become something of a spectacle. The little blonde head appeared again when he entered the hall.

"Hello," he said, waving. It remained where it was, only exposing a pair of grey eyes and a button nose. Before he could introduce himself, the little head disappeared and from what he could hear, had returned to the piano.

"I should like to collect some written statements as well as my findings, Mrs Mckinnon," he said as he put his jacket back on.

The old woman seemed flustered. "Oh," she said, looking up at him.

"Is there a problem?" he asked, raising an eyebrow.

The housekeeper wrung her hands again. "No, it is perfectly acceptable sir but um... Maggie... the maid? She can't read or write well, Inspector."

Muldoon thought for a moment. "I can write hers down, if she's happy to dictate?"

Mrs Mckinnon shook her head solemnly. "You've heard her speak, have you not? The wee lass has a terrible stutter, Inspector. She can barely string a sentence together." Mrs Mckinnon opened the basement door for him. "Anyway, I shan't stand over you," she said. He descended with footsteps that seemed to rattle the hollow wooden staircase and walked into the cramped corridor that separated their quarters. "My room is the first on the left," she called down. "What is it you're looking for down there?" she asked, leaning over the top step.

"Anything useful for my investigation, Mrs Mckinnon, but I'm afraid I can't tell you anything more."

"Understood," she said, closing the door gently.

Muldoon, finally alone, opened the first door on the left. As predicted, he found only a small room with a single bed. Behind the door was a washstand and a dresser with a modest, unframed mirror on the wall. He gently looked inside the small chest of drawers beside Violet Mckinnon's bed, finding only a few things: a bible, a crochet hook, some wool, a pair of tweezers and scissors. In a move that he was later embarrassed to have made, he opened the bible and checked for pockets or cavities where a witch may have hidden her relics. There were none. He carefully placed the things back as he found them and closed the drawers. At the foot of the bed stood an old oak trunk. Muldoon brought his handkerchief from his pocket and held it in his hand, just in case. With his other hand, he opened the lid and peered in. Amidst some clothing and a woollen shawl was a little leather-bound notebook. He flicked through it and found nothing of significance. He gently lifted the folded clothing and moved his hand across the bottom, knocking on it. Satisfied that there were no secret compartments, he closed it and sighed with relief. *The old lady's not too good to be true*, he thought.

A grey beam of light from the little window above the bed illuminated the room. He looked up at it and noticed that it sat level with the patio of the garden; he wouldn't have been able to see anything other than the passing of feet. He closed the trunk and placed his handkerchief back into his pocket.

The room directly opposite was Maggie's; unlike the house-keeper, she did not have a chest of drawers beside her bed. Behind the door was a modest mirror and a washstand. The rooms looked identical until he opened the trunk. He pushed some shawls and clothing to one side and stopped in his tracks. Surprised to see books, a heap of letters and a journal, he shot a quick glance over his shoulder. Fumbling through the en-velopes, he could see that they were all addressed to a "Margaret Ross," of five, Percy street. He opened one from the bottom of the bundle.

"Dear Maggie,

My darling sister, I have missed you so. I cannot tell you how heartbroken I was to see you go last week. Father says it is only temporary, but I do hope that you don't mind the posting. I also hope that the people are kind to you and treat you well. Please write me whenever you get the

chance. On days when I feel I am ailing, I worry
that you are ill, too. I pray for you every day.

I hope that you found the Trollope book interesting. I shall love nothing more than to hear
your thoughts.

My love, always.

Sissy."

Muldoon looked down at the copy of *Vanity Fair* in the
trunk. It was well-thumbed and had a bookmark halfway
through the pages. Stunned, he sat down on the floor and
opened some more letters.

"O' cruel world. Why should that monster take
you away from me? There are times when I wish
a storm would come and lightning strike him
down dead.

I miss you terribly.

My love, always,

Sissy."

"It is rather lonely without you here. I think I will go mad. I thoroughly enjoyed your last letter– you are so funny, but I am afraid I am too sad to laugh much these days. I cannot wait until you are home again. This house hasn't been the same since mother died. Father is grieving still, even after all this time, but he will not change his mind. You are to stay at Percy street. You must eat, Maggie. I know it is hard—I feel your anguish too, but we must believe that this isn't forever.

Psalm 34:18

The Lord is near to the brokenhearted and saves the crushed in spirit.

My love, always,

Sissy."

Muldoon stared out at the tiny basement window for a moment, contemplating. Contrary to what Violet Mckinnon had just told him, the stuttering Maggie could read and write well—at least, Margaret Ross could. He looked back down at the letters and observed the sender's address, which baffled him all the more. Maggie had not revealed herself to be a witch or a fan of the occult, and shouldn't have stirred any suspicion, but all evidence had to be collected. He removed one letter from the stack and stuffed it in his breast pocket and piled the others together, tying the cord around them. He returned them to the trunk and closed the lid. Standing up again, he looked about the room with a finality and hoped to find more secrets upstairs.

On second thought, he appreciated that the ground floor of the house, made lovely by the tinkling of a piano, felt open and more welcoming than the small, whitewashed servants quarters. Seeing that the door of the drawing room was open, he followed the trail of music and began the next phase of his investigation.

Sitting at the piano in the far corner of the room was a little, ringlet-headed girl of four or five years old, tapping the keys with her tiny pink tongue poking out of her mouth. Muldoon smiled at the sight of such a small person playing such a large instrument. Behind the child, a mousy-haired governess sat in the armchair, bent over her sewing. Her face, slightly shadowed by the manner in which she held her head, emphasised the curves of her lovely cheeks, nose, and the fullness of her lips.

Having entered the room unseen and with the efficiency of a cat, he stepped back against the sideboard and waited for the music to finish. When the child stopped, she turned to look at him and stared.

"Bravo," he said, clapping gently. The governess almost leapt out of her chair and on seeing the inspector, stuffed her sewing in the basket beside her and stood to attention.

"Inspector," she said, "how can we help you?"

Sarah Jones was tall, with a heart-shaped face and pale skin that—on that particular day—looked even more ashen in the grey light of the cloudy morning. Muldoon smiled, revealing his dimples. "I'm conducting my investigation, Miss?"

"Jones," she said as a tint of pink blushed her cheeks. "I'm Sarah Jones." She approached him, paused for a moment and decided to hold her hand out. He shook it gently.

"I'm Daniel Muldoon."

"Is this about..." Sarah quickly turned to look at the little girl who was watching them with an expression of fascination and turned back to Muldoon. "My mistress?" she whispered. Muldoon nodded.

"I'm just looking about the house for now, but I will be looking to speak with you by the end of the day."

Sarah nodded. "Very well. Elsie has her tea at four. I should be able to speak with you then."

"Are you a doctor?" asked the little girl, interrupting the conversation. Her governess gave her a scolding look but Muldoon laughed it off.

"Me? No, dear."

"Mary says you've come to make Mummy better."

Muldoon looked at the child for a moment and then back at the governess, whose complexion had faded from pale to deathly white. "She says things, Inspector," she said nervously. "We surmised that it must be an imaginary friend."

"Mary is not imaginary. She's here!"

"Elsie, my darling," Sarah said, "Please go and ask Mrs Mckinnon for a bun. You've earned a treat after all that piano practice."

They watched the little girl climb down from the piano stool and skip to the door, where she stopped and looked at them for a moment with a piercing gaze that rendered her governess silent until she left the room. "Things haven't been the same since, you know..." Sarah said, looking away. "The little one says things all the time. I never know what to believe."

"Is that so?"

"All the time, but every now and then, I'll feel a chill pass through me and she'll know all about it. She says 'that's only Mary' and continues to play with her toys or read her books." Muldoon looked down at Sarah's bitten fingernails as she spoke. "I've known Elsie since she was a baby, Inspector. She grows stranger every day, talking to this... *Mary* and stopping mid-sentence when I walk into the room, as though I have interrupted their conversation." She shook her head and laughed. "Listen to me. I'm foolish. She's just a child."

"Children can sometimes speak strangely. They're often used as vessels, Miss Jones. It's not unreasonable to be afraid of their strange behaviour."

Sarah looked him in the eye. "Vessels for what?"

"That's what I'm here to find out, Miss Jones—are you all right?"

"If you'll just excuse me," she said, turning away and desperately reaching for the door handle. Muldoon lunged forward and caught her as she stumbled.

"Steady there," he said, scooping her up. He laid her down on the nearest sofa and removed his jacket. "I'll get you something." He quickly poured a glass of brandy from the drinks cabinet and handed it to Sarah, who took it from him with a trembling hand.

"I'm so sorry, I felt so light-headed all of a sudden."

Muldoon sat down in a chair opposite and regarded her for a moment. The dark rings under her eyes told him that she hadn't slept in days, and he had noticed her wide-eyed horror when

Elsie spoke of Mary. He encouraged her to sip the drink and leaned forward. "We don't have to speak today," he said quietly, pulling a card out of his pocket. "I'll leave you my address."

After Sarah had reassured him that she was well enough to stand, Muldoon left her resting on the sofa and returned to the hallway for the remainder of the investigation, passing Maggie on his way to the parlour room. She looked down at the floor and scuttled past him like a mouse, disappearing again into the back kitchen with her cleaning bucket and rag. His observation was interrupted by the striking of the grandfather clock behind him, calling for his attention. He approached it slowly, reading the numbers on the clock face. It was twelve o'clock.

Compelled by a force he hadn't noticed before, he touched the wood of the clock until a sharp, hot sting shot through his fingertips all the way into his gut, forcing him to pull his hand away: danger. He fixed his eyes on the swinging pendulum that glided back and forth in harmony with the beating of his heart until it slowed completely. The hallway around him darkened to a point where he could only make out his warm breath in sub-zero temperatures, and transformed to a candle-lit hallway. When he looked at the glass around the door, the sky outside had blackened. In the corner of his eye, a shadow moved away from him, walking toward the stairs. He turned to look at the woman being dragged up the stairs by her feet. Her eyes, dead and hollow, stared right at him as he followed the trail of blood to the staircase. Her long, chestnut hair draped like a train as her head rolled over each step and hit the lip with a bump. Muldoon stepped forward to follow and narrowed his eyes. The body was being dragged up the stairs by a man with no face.

17

"INSPECTOR, IS EVERYTHING ALL right?"

Muldoon snapped out of his trance and fixed his gaze on the ruddy face of Violet Mckinnon. She had her hand on his sleeve. "Can I get you something?"

He shook his head. "Thank you, Mrs McKinnon. I'll be fine."

She slowly removed her hand and stepped back, studying his greyed face. "As long as you're sure? You were staring into the abyss there."

"I was, was I?" he asked, forcing a smile. "I don't know what came over me. His head throbbed. "What time is it?"

"Why it's twelve o' clock, Inspector. Well, a minute past if we want to be particular."

"Still?" He looked at the clock once more.

"I know. Time's running away with me and all! I'll be back in the kitchen if you need me." She turned on her heel and headed to the back of the house.

"Mrs Mckinnon," he called, staring at the clock again. The housekeeper turned to look at him from across the hall. "This clock here, is it working?"

She tilted her head in bafflement as they both watched the long hand move clockwise across its face, ticking quietly as it always did. "Yes, Inspector. I should think that it is, why?"

Muldoon stepped back from the clock and regarded it again. "Nothing. It's nothing. Thank you."

Alone again, he stood back by the front door and folded his arms, watching. The carpeted stairs that had just been coated in a woman's blood were clean. There was nobody in the hallway. Unable to move any further from the vision replaying in his mind, he stepped outside for a cigarette.

Standing on the front step, he admired the view of the street; it was quiet, but there was enough life passing by in the form of coaches, pedestrians and wagons. He walked down into the front garden and looked back at the house. Elsie Bryant's face appeared in the parlour room window, staring at him. He made his best attempt to wave in a friendly manner, but she didn't wave back. Instead she put her finger to her mouth, her lips forming the "shhhh" shape. Not knowing what to do about her stare, Muldoon simply smiled. She disappeared from view, easing his discomfort. Still halfway through his cigarette, he decided to explore the side of the house and the back garden. The tall wooden gate opened with a simple push of the spring latch. He stepped into the garden and closed it behind him.

Beside the house was a simple gravel path, forking off to a stairway that led to the basement and a modest garden straight ahead, with patio furniture and decorative shrubs. At the back of the walled garden was a simple brick outhouse. He approached it and had a tug at the wooden door: locked. The padlock looked old and appeared speckled with rust, but it was still too tough for a man without a key or a bag of tools. He moved to the side of the structure and looked in through the cobwebbed window. There wasn't much to see inside apart from some garden tools and a few refuse sacks along the back wall. He stepped back and took another drag of his cigarette, looking up at the house again, fixing his eye on the back kitchen and then down to the basement.

He remained still, and watched Maggie go into the back kitchen and hang out some white laundry. She was rolling them through a mangle before awkwardly pegging them to the line. He studied her as she held out shirts and nightgowns.

Margaret Ross was a fine actress, and he didn't trust her at all.

Later, when Muldoon had finished his fruitless inspection of the downstairs rooms, he found himself loitering outside the parlour room door. The sound of piano music had beckoned him to return and listen. As was his way, he slid into the room with the stealthiness of a prowling cat and took a seat in the corner, unnoticed. This time, the pianist played with the confidence of a player much older than four. She looked lovely in the low light of the mid-morning; she wore a simple dress of green muslin, but he felt she didn't need much in order to warrant attention.

Sarah was playing something he found beautiful but didn't recognise; he was intrigued and sat down on the sofa where she had been lying when he last saw her. She played with conviction, and he admired her skill as he waited patiently for her to finish. The colour had returned to her face and for a moment, he could have believed that the previous incident hadn't happened at all.

"What are you playing?" he asked when she finished and rested her hands on her lap.

"Elgar. Salut d'Amour."

Muldoon, embarrassed by his lack of musical ear or a fluency in French, nodded. "It sounds lovely," he said.

Sarah smiled warmly. "He hasn't been composing long. I'm not surprised you haven't heard of him." She looked down at her lap, not knowing what else to say.

He took a deep breath and released it, along with his hesitation to speak. "I'm sorry for what I said, Miss Jones." She lifted her head to read him. He cleared his throat. "About what I said—you know—vessels. I shouldn't have said that. It was insensitive of me."

"That's quite all right."

"No, it's not, Miss Jones. I should know better than to say such things about a child you so clearly love."

Her eyes were glassy with tears as she listened to him speak. She swallowed and said, "Please tell me she's not in danger."

"I can't say that for sure. She's not possessed, however. That's all I know."

Sarah sobbed into her hands. Muldoon clenched his jaw and sat there for a moment before deciding to stand over her and place a hand on her shoulder. "Try not to worry, Miss Jones. I'll get to the bottom of this." He didn't know if he could, or would, but a woman's tears were a powerful weapon, whether she meant to use them or not. He thought it best to be optimistic.

She wiped her tears away with her handkerchief and stood up. "I'm sorry. It has been a very difficult time, Inspector."

"I understand."

Before they could say any more, Elsie burst into the room with her doll, Blissy in her arms. "Sorry I'm late. I was playing," she said.

Sarah, not knowing if she had told Elsie to come back or not, smiled and opened her arms. Elsie ran into them and embraced Sarah, directing her eyes toward Muldoon. "We should go to the park, Elsie," Sarah said, stroking the little girl's hair. "We haven't gone for a walk today. How would you like that? We should get some fresh air."

"I would like to see the ducks again, and go to the Fairy Glen."

"Then we shall. We shall. Go and get your coat, darling." Sarah sniffed and wiped her eyes once more. The blotches on her skin from her fit of tears had refreshed her complexion. "Inspector, will you need anything more from me today?"

"I don't think so, Miss Jones. I will be coming back tomorrow anyway for—"

Sarah raised a hand to silence him. "Then I have something you might want to see before you do," she said. "I'll be back in a moment."

Sarah returned promptly, placing a bundle of letters on Muldoon's lap. "What's this?" he asked, bemused.

"They're from Mrs Bryant to Mr Bryant. She asked me to post them but we have no address for Mr Bryant, so I kept them safe for her."

His eyes narrowed. "Why is there no address?"

"I... I don't know," she said. "I supposed that Mrs Bryant may have lost it or that he didn't write. I really don't know."

"Is Mr Bryant well?"

"I think so. We haven't received *anything* to suggest otherwise."

Muldoon flicked through the envelopes. "This is a lot of letters. How long has Mr Bryant been away?"

Sarah thought for a moment and tucked some loose hair behind her ear. "It must have been... about two months by now? He went to South Africa."

"What for?"

"Business. He works in the goldfields—well, he doesn't mine any more but I think it is some sort of..." She blushed. "I have no idea, truth be told. I'm not... it's not really any of my business. I've hardly ever spoken with Mr Bryant." Muldoon watched the realisation sink into her face. "I suppose I don't really know him."

Muldoon cleared his throat. "It's not unusual for a governess to not know much about her employers, Miss Jones."

"But you see, Inspector Muldoon, it is in this case." Sarah sat beside him on the sofa. "I've worked for the family for almost four years and Mrs Bryant has been a good friend to me. I cared for her and the baby—Elsie—when Frances was alone. He went off to Australia to find their fortune and she had nobody."

"Not even her mother?"

Sarah shook her head vehemently. "No, you see—Mrs Larkin and the late Mr Larkin didn't approve of the union with Mr Bryant," she said, watching the door as she spoke. Muldoon listened intently. "They didn't like him, but Frances married him anyway. They didn't speak, and when John left for Australia, she had no one."

"Seems a bit harsh," Muldoon said.

Sarah didn't seem to notice the comment and kept talking. "He sent her some money to find a nanny, and she found me. I'd do anything for this family, but there has been no opportunity for me to really get to know Mr Bryant's character."

"I see," Muldoon said, crossing his legs.

"Sorry, I don't know why I went into detail with that. I just—I suppose you brought something to my attention. I don't doubt that Mr Bryant is as kind and fair as Mrs Bryant, if that's what you are wanting to know. It's really none of my business, but Frances is a friend to me and I can't think why she doesn't have an address for him."

"it is unusual," Muldoon muttered in agreement.

Sarah stood up again and straightened her skirts before reaching for her green hat that waited on the table. "Anyway, Inspector," she said, adjusting it neatly in the mirror. Muldoon thought that Miss Jones had the perfect head for a hat, with a fine little chin and a long, swan-like neck. She turned to face him once more. "If there is anything more you need of me, I will be here tomorrow."

"Miss Jones," he said as she reached for the door handle. "Have you read any of these letters?"

She seemed hurt by the question, and leaned against the door. "Heavens, no! I would never, Inspector. I swear on my life."

"Very well. Thank you, Miss Jones."

She left silently. Muldoon looked down at the stack of letters again and heard the front door close with a click. The house, having endured some brief excitement and activity, fell back into a deep slumber, its signs of life only evident by the ticking of the clocks.

18

30th September, 1892

Dear John,

We are having a seance tonight. I want to end this madness. Elsie is saying terrifying things again about this Mary woman. Only this morning, I asked her who she was playing with and she said "Mary" again!

She told mother that she sees things in her room. I fear that if this house is haunted, it is by more than one ghost. I imagine you laughing as you read this.

I was as sceptical as you are until mother said that there is a man in the nursery. He watches Sarah while she sleeps.

Elsie is something of a little liar, though. She can be a wicked child. Those dolls, it must be the dolls. Why does she lie to me so? I will burn every single one of them.

You're going to wake me up tomorrow and in-form me that this is all a dream.

Sincerely,

Your loving madwoman.

4th October, 1892

Dear John,

The seance was the strangest thing. I can see why they are so popular in high society! Mother, Mr Kingsley and a solicitor called Fred... oh forgive me, I cannot remember his name. Wilcox, I think. Anyway, we conducted this meeting as per Mr Kingsley's rules and it was riveting. Not only did the flames of the candles misbehave but when Mary appeared across the table, the glass smashed to smithereens. She's petrified, but I don't know of what. I told everybody what I saw, what I felt and what I thought. Mother suggested that I should seek some rest, so I did. Then, oddly, when I woke the following morning and wanted to continue the investigation, she said no!

Nobody will tell me why they are so unsettled.

Oh, I hear the scratching again. Mary used to scratch the walls when he wouldn't let her out.

I had the strangest dream, John. Am I Mary? Are you trapping me here, John? Where are you?

Sincerely,

Your loving madwoman.

15th October, 1892

Dear John,

This house is strange. It feels like it doesn't belong to me. I know you say I'm a madwoman, and perhaps I am, but you must listen to me. Those ornaments in the parlour room—they move around. Maggie swears she doesn't move them and I was so embarrassed to find them exactly where I'd left them this time. It's as though they're playing tricks on me. I cannot prove anything.

And the walls, John. It's as though we have rats. Mrs Mckinnon asked the rat catcher to come at my request and he found nothing, but I still hear the scratching, the shuffling, the dragging. They must have a nest in the walls and under the floorboards. It keeps me up all night!

Mother doesn't believe me. She has been overly concerned since the seance. How ridiculous she is!

I do worry, John. I'm worried not just for myself but for Elsie. I'm worried because I'm going to die here, John. Please come home.

Your beloved madwoman,

Frances.

28th of October, 1892

Dear John,

Please come home. I don't give a damn about Mr
Ellman– I need you here with *me*. Tell me where
he is and I shall go to him myself. He has no right
to keep you from me.

Mary reached out and touched me. A few weeks
ago now, Mr Kingsley did come. We *did* have a
seance. I am so very sorry that I did not laugh
with you. I should have said no. But Mary told
me everything—well, she can't 'tell' me but she
shows me. It's not safe here, but nobody believes me. Swinson gives me tonic upon tonic and
won't let me out! Mother listens to him. She cannot look at me without crying. I assure her that
there is nothing wrong, but she cannot believe
me.

They won't let me see Elsie, John. They won't let
me see her.

I have nothing else to do but pace my bed-room, drink tonic, cod liver oil and swallow these wicked tablets that he says I need. The way he looks at me is so patronising. I loathe this man. Come home. Please, please. I need you. Forgive the delay in my response. These tablets, they put me to sleep, but I'm not really asleep. I see every-thing. Mary comes here. He comes here. I don't like him watching me.

Why do you visit me in my dreams but not when I wake? It has surely been months now.

What Mary says about you cannot be true. The other night, I read your letter. I imagined you were speaking to me as I read it and it comforted me so, but you must understand that I was as torn as the paper that rested on the table. I ripped it up, but that wasn't the strangest thing. When I returned to the table, the pieces had been re-arranged, and they said:

He Will Kill You All

Who is He, John? Why does he mean to kill me?
Please help me. I am lost.

Your Frances

10th November 1892

Dear John,

I got out. Nobody knows. They all went out for
the morning on various errands. Only mother
was here and she was asleep. It was my fault. I
had been up all night screaming and shouting
because you are here but I cannot reach you. I
understand now—you are trying to reach me. I
hear you on the landing. I see you through the
keyhole. I hear you scratching in the walls.

Are you dead, my love? Do you need me to come
to you?

> *Last night as I lay on my*
> *pillow,*

> *Last night as I lay on my*
> *bed,*

> *Last night as I lay on my*
> *pillow,*

> *I dreamed that my Bon-*
> *nie was dead.*

If you are not dead, you must come back to me
and end this madness. I will surely die if you
don't. This is torment. I will die if you don't
come back, John. Perhaps I am already dead.

They think I can't hear them as I lie there. They say I shall have to go to a special hospital if I don't recover. Recover from what? There is nothing the matter with me. I have tried with all my will to tell them what has happened here but they think me mad. Stop playing games and come home.

Anyway, I climbed to the attic. Mary showed me the way. I slipped into the entrance. It was so dark, but the potpourri was comforting and I slid the panel with ease. The little staircase is rather cold, but the room remains usable. There she was, on her hands and knees, looking right at me. Early morning light was trying its best to shine through the bricked up windows, and I could make her out clearly. I bet she was beautiful once. She stared at me with these sad, doll-like eyes and bountiful waves of chestnut hair hung from her face. She cannot speak, what with her throat being cut but she can touch things and move things. She lifted the lid of a chest beside her and passed me a razor. I believe I fainted after that.

Some time after, I found my way back downstairs. Mother was looking for me on the ground
floor and Mrs Mckinnon had just returned. I lay
in my bed and pulled the covers up.

If he comes for me, I have the razor now.

He is the spider; we are the flies. Evil crawls where
we cannot reach it, and watches through the gaps
in the walls. This isn't my house.

Your beloved wife, Frances.

MULDOON DROPPED THE LETTERS into a box and closed the
lid when he heard a firm knock at the door. "Come in," he said.

Mae Magnusson strode into the room, her bustle bouncing
behind her as she turned and closed the door with a quick slam.

"Mae, how lovely it is to see you," Muldoon said. He was
leaning back in his chair with his feet crossed over the desk. In

one hand was a cigarette and in the other, a tumbler of scotch. Mae raised an eyebrow.

"I hope you haven't bought those cigarettes with your rent money."

"Absolutely not." Muldoon placed the scotch back on the desk and sat up. With his cigarette in his mouth, he pulled out the desk drawer with his right hand and extracted a chunky envelope. "I always have rent."

"You're late this week, Daniel."

"And very sorry about that I am," he said, taking a drag of his cigarette. "Say, Mae, would you like one?"

She took the envelope from him and stuffed it into a pocket in her skirt. "How much have you had to drink, Muldoon?"

"Only enough to feel a bit relaxed, Mae. I was meaning the cigarette but you can have a scotch, too."

"The cigarette will do fine, thank you."

He removed the case from his pocket and opened it, holding it out for her to choose one. With long, slim fingers she took one from the case. "Matches are just there," Muldoon said, nodding at the matchbox at the end of the desk. She took a match and ignited it on the first strike, her face aglow in the quickening flame. Mae had been a pretty young woman, once. The sharp lines around her lips deepened as she drew in the smoke. Her brown eyes, once bright and feline, drooped slightly like those of a basset hound.

"You look like you've had a day," she said, perching on the edge of the desk.

"It's been unusual, to say the least." Muldoon looked at his landlady with tired eyes.

"What has that Gill got you doing now?" she asked. It was no secret that Gill was one of Mae's least favourite people.

"Ghosts, Mae."

She threw her head back with a cackle. "What next? Ghosts?"

"It's quite interesting, actually," he mused, blowing smoke out of the corner of his mouth. "There's definitely a mystery, but I don't think it's as simple as ghosts." Their eyes met. "I had a vision."

"Oh aye?" Mae looked down at him with her heavy, velvety eyelids and flicked some ash into the ashtray.

"Someone was murdered there. Some poor lass I don't know the name of."

"It's a murder case then? What's it got to do with you?"

"Well, that's the thing, Mae. Until we find a body, it's just me and my visions. Can't take that to court. So far I've got the letters of a madwoman, a strange child, a maid who seems to be lying through her teeth, a missing husband, and a body somewhere."

"I wouldn't want to be you today," she said, smiling. Muldoon laughed.

"You sure you don't want a break from the punters?"

"No." She shook her head and flashed him a seductive smile. "My work doesn't follow me home, darlin'. Besides, one of the perks of being as old as I am is that you spend more time counting money than anything else."

"Surely you still get customers, Mae?"

"That's very kind of you," she said with an amused grin. "One or two, but I'm as old as the hills. I bet some of them would feel like they were shagging their mother, you know?"

"I don't, personally," he said, shaking his head, "but I see what you mean."

"Speaking of which, I'd better get back." She stood up and stubbed out the cigarette. "Goodnight, Daniel."

"Goodnight, Mae."

Mae closed the door behind her and returned upstairs. Muldoon opened the box again. Reading the ramblings of Frances Bryant wore his eyes out, tiring his mind with every word. He didn't know if her letters were intended to be riddles, but he read them as such. After some time, he lifted out the last letter and began to read until his concentration was broken by the movement in the corner of his office. He lifted his eyes from his work and saw only an oilskin hanging from the door's hook. It was nothing. He returned to France Bryant's letter. It read:

"She can only scream when he takes what isn't his."

Lowering the letter from his face, he found himself within an inch of the face of a dead woman, paralysing him with her stare. With sunken, dead eyes, she held him there. He watched the lifeless, white lips open into a blood-red chasm. The scream that came from it pierced his ears, vibrated through his skull and made his teeth ache. "Jesus!" he exclaimed, falling backwards in the small, rickety chair he was sitting on. Rolling out of the fall, he stood up quickly, his heart pounding, and looked around the room breathlessly. He was alone. Muldoon grabbed the tumbler containing the last dregs of scotch and with a shaking hand, poured himself another.

19

BEATRICE LARKIN OPENED THE door to Muldoon when he returned to Percy Street the following morning. He immediately noticed her swollen, red eyes that she'd tried to fan with her handkerchief behind the door. "Inspector Muldoon!" she said, sounding surprised. "Thank you for coming. I'm Beatrice Larkin—Frances' mother."

Muldoon stepped forward and wiped his feet on the mat. The rain outside pelted the windows, washing the world clean as it rolled down the crevices between cobbles in shallow streams. The light from the candles and lamps in the hall glowed with a welcoming warmth as he hung his hat and coat on the stand. "Inspector, you're soaked," Beatrice remarked, looking at his dripping overcoat.

"That's just the coat, Mrs Larkin. I am all right, thank you." His hands, red and throbbing, briefly found some warmth in his pockets before he realised he was being rude and brought them back out.

Beatrice rushed to the first door on the right and gestured for him to follow. "We should go into the parlour room and sit by the fire."

"Thank you."

Entering the parlour room, the warmth of the fire smoth-
ered him with its heat, crackling in the hearth. His wet, damp
clothing had become a thing of the past as he felt his skin flush
in accordance with the temperature. He was suddenly overcome with a comfortable feeling of drowsiness as the deepening
warmth of the air penetrated the chill in his bones. He looked
down at the fire: there was enough coal in it to warm a docker's
family for a week.

They sat down on the white sofas, separated by a Queen
Anne coffee table. Muldoon desperately stifled a yawn while
Mrs Larkin picked up the lace tablecloth and placed it down
again gracefully, ironing out any creases with her hands. Although blotchy from the crying, Beatrice was a good-look-
ing woman, with greying blonde hair and hooded, blue eyes.
"Would you mind waiting until after the meeting for tea? It's
just that..." Beatrice put her hand to her bottom lip to steady it.
"Mrs Mckinnon is with Frances right now. I thought I should
make myself available in time for your arrival."

"It's no bother, Mrs Larkin."

She relaxed slightly, resting her hands on her lap. Muldoon
leaned forward. "Mrs Larkin, I read some of Frances' letters last
night."

Mrs Larkin turned pale. "Oh God," she said.

"You knew about the letters, then?"

She nodded with her hand on her mouth again, waited a moment, and took a deep breath before speaking. "I told her to give them to Sarah but... there was no address for Mr Bryant."

Muldoon sat back, feeling energised by the revelation. "Why do you think there was no address, Mrs Bryant?"

"I don't know." She looked in his direction, almost through him. "I fear the worst."

"What do you mean?"

"I should have trusted my instincts. I thought I was wrong but... it looks terrible, doesn't it?"

"I'm not sure I follow, Mrs Larkin."

Her eyes flitted around the room until they returned to Muldoon. "The ghost? What if? What if John Bryant is..."

She froze, leaving the rest of her sentence to float away into the air between them. Muldoon looked right to the blazing fire for a minute and when he accepted that she wasn't going to continue, he prodded. "What if John Bryant is what, Mrs Larkin?"

"Nothing." She shook her head and sniffed. "Take no notice of me. I have no reason to say that." She wrung her handkerchief in her hands. He watched her mind wander away from the room and suddenly reappear in the form of a gasp. "Frances—you need to see Frances, is that right?"

"That would be helpful, yes."

She dabbed her eyes and took a deep breath. "Very well."

Beatrice stopped outside a closed door on the first floor landing. Muldoon decided to hold back and stand on the top step.

She knocked on the door gently and waited until it opened slowly and revealed the anxious face of Mrs Mckinnon. She looked from Beatrice to Muldoon and nodded, opening the door slightly wider to let them in. Her eyes were alert, and she didn't smile in her usual way. Muldoon silently followed Beatrice into the large, well-lit bedroom, furnished with chintz and mahogany. To his surprise, the natural light had been blocked by the closed curtains. The room, despite the potpourri and flickering candles, made him feel as though he had been summoned to keep watch over a body.

He blinked as he studied the surroundings. The carpet felt like soft clouds under his feet as he tentatively walked over to the bed with Beatrice.

For a second, he thought he had seen a corpse, but the weak blinking of the darkened eyelids assured him otherwise. On the bed lay a thin female figure with matted hair; her chest heaved and sank with a rattling breath. Muldoon noticed that her hands were bound to the bed posts and she stared vacantly at the ceiling. He narrowed his eyes when he saw her face: it was so ghostly, that he couldn't be sure he hadn't seen her before. He was reminded of the apparition that had frightened him in his office, knocking him out of his chair with her sudden appearance. He tried to think of the face again but the appearance of Frances' face was too distracting. "Mrs Bryant?" he asked gently. Beatrice turned to look at him and smiled weakly.

"This is Frances, yes."

Not wanting to spend a minute longer in the room, Mrs Mckinnon bowed and shuffled out, closing the door firmly behind her.

"Would you like to speak to her?" Beatrice asked nervously.

"If that's possible?" asked Muldoon, looking at the tray of pill-bottles beside the bed.

Beatrice stepped back and gestured at the chair at Frances' right. He sat down slowly, as though too much noise would cause her to spring out of the bed and attack him. He had visited asylums before, but he had also visited the sickbed, and Mrs Bryant presented him with a unique mix of the two atmospheres. "Hello, Frances," he said.

Muldoon was surprised to see the woman move. He thought of the photograph Gill had shown him. *She doesn't look like that at the moment.* The woman's face, as gaunt as it was, turned to look at him. Her eyes, dark and sunken, lifted to meet his. At first, she seemed ready to say something, but her mouth closed as quickly as it had opened. Muldoon ran his tongue across his back teeth and thought of what to say next. Observing her thin, bruised wrists and ankles, he turned to Beatrice. "Why is she restrained, Mrs Larkin?"

"Doctor's orders, Inspector. So she doesn't do herself any harm."

"Harm?"

Beatrice lowered her voice to a whisper. "There was a razor under her pillow, Inspector. We... we thought she meant to do herself harm."

I have the razor now.

Frances groaned and with her pale, cracked lips, mouthed something. Muldoon leaned forward to listen. "Water," he said. "She needs some water, Mrs Larkin."

Beatrice fetched the pitcher from the sideboard and brought it over to Muldoon, who had retrieved a glass from her bedside table. She poured it and set the pitcher down, bringing her hands under Frances' head to lift it. Muldoon carefully tilted the glass against her bottom lip. She gulped it greedily as it flowed down the corners of her mouth and into her hair; she didn't take her eyes off Muldoon. When she stopped drinking, he gently pulled it away from her.

"Who are you?" she asked in a hoarse voice.

"I'm Inspector Daniel Muldoon, Frances. I'm here to help you."

There was a pause before she coughed and said, "you cannot help me." Beatrice gently laid her daughter's head back onto the pillow and stepped back with a trembling bottom lip. Frances turned her face away to look at the drawn window. "No one can help me."

"I think I can." He reached into his pocket and presented her with a small wooden crucifix.

"Dear Lord," she said, shaking her head weakly, "not you as well." Her eyes rolled away and back to him, demonstrably fatigued.

"What do you mean, Frances?"

"You don't see what I see," she said, releasing a deep breath. "Nobody does. They think I'm insane. Or in your case," she coughed drily a few times, "possessed."

Muldoon cleared his throat. "I'm going to hold this to your head and say a few words," he said, wiping some sweat from his forehead with the back of his free hand. "Priests usually just crack on with it with barely a word, but I'd like to give you the courtesy of explaining what's going on," he said gently. "May I?"

She said nothing, and with a look of indignation, nodded once. She heard the words roll from his mouth in softly spoken Latin. When he had finished, he sat back and sighed with relief. Nothing had happened. The room fell into a hush that was characterised only by the sniffling of Beatrice Larkin.

"Mother," Frances said with a new found interest in Muldoon, powered by annoyance. "Leave us, please."

Beatrice stopped immediately and looked at the inspector, who said, "it's all right, Mrs Larkin. She can't hurt me."

"I'll be right outside, Inspector."

The sobbing resumed on the other side of the closed door. Frances rolled her eyes in irritation.

"Speak candidly, Inspector," she said, coughing slightly as the air caught the back of her throat again. "Why were you brought here?"

Muldoon thought for a moment, and spoke softly. "There are those close to you who want you to be well, Frances. They worry that there are forces of evil contributing to your current state of being."

She raised an eyebrow. "Bravo."

"I read your letters, Mrs Bryant. They were meant for—"

"John!" Her face brightened immediately, as the mention of his name forced a rush of blood through the top layer of her skin. "Where is he?"

Muldoon shook his head. "I'm afraid I don't know, Mrs Bryant."

He watched her tragically sink back into a malaise and look away. "I am in hell, aren't I?"

"No, I don't think so."

"Then why are you here?" she snapped. "Why are you sticking that crucifix in my face?"

"I... I had to rule it out—"

"Distrust."

Muldoon, taken aback by the accusation, found his face flush with the heat of embarrassment. "Procedure, Mrs Bryant. There are things about this situation that... they cannot be explained. I thought that, perhaps—"

"Perhaps I'm evil instead of mad!"

"If you'd let me finish, Mrs Bryant..." Muldoon said sternly. "I could explain."

Her eyes widened, and looked away in shame "Forgive me. I am out of practice."

"Well," Muldoon said as he put the crucifix away, "now that we understand each other, perhaps we can solve this mystery. What do you think?"

"It depends," she said, licking her visibly dry lips.

Muldoon looked at the ties and back to her face. "Depends on what?"

"Whether you believe me."

"Let's start again. I'm Inspector Muldoon and I am here to help you. I promise to listen to everything you tell me. I am here to review the case. I am not the judge. How's that?"

For the first time, she smiled. He spied a glint in her eye: hope. "I've seen her too, Frances," he said reassuringly.

Frances remained still, as though he had asked her to freeze so that he could paint her portrait. "You have?"

"Yes. I've seen Mary, Frances."

"Where did you see her?"

"On the stairs. Where do you see her?"

"Everywhere."

"Could you—?"

They were interrupted by an abrupt knock on the door. Muldoon stood up and waited for the door to open. Frances watched in terror as a doctor's bag appeared, followed by Dr Swinson and Beatrice, who had finally stopped crying.

"Good morning!" The older man beamed as he reached out a hand for Muldoon. "I'm Dr Swinson. Mrs Bryant is due for her medication and, as it was rather quiet in the surgery this morning, I thought I'd pop in and see to her before my afternoon house calls."

Muldoon looked from the doctor to Frances. "Of course, doctor. May I ask how long this appointment will take?"

"As long as it needs to!" Swinson said. Both men stared at one another for a second before Swinson broke into jovial laughter, rubbing his round belly for added measure. Muldoon laughed along nervously and looked back at Frances. He didn't know her well enough to read her, but he knew people, and the arrival of Dr Swinson certainly didn't warrant a smile.

The doctor walked over to the sideboard, opened his bag and started to rummage for his apparatus when Muldoon heard a sharp whisper come from Frances. He attentively went to her and leaned in to listen.

"When you said those Latin words... what was that?" she asked, her eyes darting to the doctor who was still busy with his bag.

"A prayer to St Michael, to protect you from evil."

She looked at him and smiled. A single tear rolled down her cheek.

Muldoon left the room and loitered on the landing, caught between descent for a cigarette break or ascent to further investigate. The decision was made for him when he heard the heavy footsteps of a child running around upstairs, but something in the guest room drew his attention. He thought he saw a shadow pass across the open doorway.

Draping his blazer on the banister, he crept slowly toward the open door of the other bedroom. "Hello?" he asked, poking his head into the room. The bed in the centre of it was neatly made with a delicate crochet lace blanket brightening the plum-coloured aesthetic. It was more modest than the master bedroom, with a single wardrobe and a smaller mahogany dresser in the corner, but his eyes darted to the dressmaker's dummy in front of the window. He wondered if the straw-stuffed body was the cause of the shadow, and looked around again. Like the other rooms, this one also had a chest at the foot of the bed. He checked to see if anyone was behind him and knelt down in front of it. It was far more ornate than the ones belonging to the servant's quarters, with a heavier lid. Just as he was about to unlock the clasp, he heard gurgling and let go. The curtain twitched slightly in the corner of his eye. He went to it, and paused for a moment, staring at the chintz fabric for more movement. Grabbing the edge, he swiftly pulled it back. Nothing. He did notice that the window was open slightly, and realising that it must have been a draught, closed it. The gurgling sound continued, this time from under the bed. Like a snake charmer approaching a wild cobra, he approached the edge of the bed with caution, and got down on his hands and knees. He held his breath and pulled the cover up. Nothing. He sighed a breath of relief and hung his head for a second.

Returning to the chest, he unlocked the clasp and lifted it.

Muldoon gasped at the sight of blood; his own ran cold. Everything in the box was soaked in fresh, copper-scented scarlet. His eyes moved up from the drenched linens and that's when he saw it. The eyes of the dead woman met his. He froze: it was the face he had seen the night before. Her neck gaped open, slashed viciously. He could do nothing but stare into her lifeless eyes until he felt her hands reach up and grab his collar. Her pale, dead lips moved up and down, akin to a landed fish, in a desperate attempt to speak. He fell backwards, freeing himself from her desperate grasp.

Rubbing his eyes, he scrabbled up from his position and looked again at the chest: only clothes, jewellery and shoes rested where he had just seen a woman in red, horribly contorted and looking right at him. "Jesus," he sighed. "You're in my head, girl."

He sat for a short while on the floor, looking directly at the chest that just minutes before, had a woman crawling out of it, intent on grabbing his attention. Her neck came to mind as he remembered the words *I have the razor now.* "Where are you, Mary?" he asked quietly. The sound of footsteps upstairs compelled him to forget about the box, stand up and continue with the investigation.

20

LITTLE ELSIE BRYANT WAS playing in the nursery when Muldoon knocked gently on the door. Sarah opened it and judging by her face, seemed relieved to see him. "Inspector," she said, holding a bundle of linens in her arms. "I was just tidying up in here. How can I help you?"

"I thought I'd have a look at the nursery while the doctor is visiting Mrs Bryant."

"Of course," she said, walking back into the room. She placed the linens in one of the large dressers and started picking up toys. "Just let me get these things out of the way." A line of dolls had been assembled across the room from the wardrobe to the bed.

"No!" called Elsie from the far end of the room. "Those are my maids."

"Elsie, the Inspector needs to look around the room and—"

The child darted over to the dolls and tried to shield them from Sarah with her body. "Mary needs pretty maids all in a row!"

"Elsie!" Sarah commanded, standing up straight. The child dropped to her knees and began to wail.

"Elsie," Sarah said again, through her teeth this time. "Stop with the foolish behaviour, now. Or there'll be no supper."

The child continued to wail, pausing only to release a high pitched scream with a beetroot face. Sarah grabbed an arm and forced her to stand on her feet but she wrestled out of her governess' grip and fled the room. Muldoon, not wanting to collide with the furious, miniature fugitive, stepped aside and let her pass. "Elsie!" Sarah called, readjusting the hair that had come loose in the struggle. She stopped and let a doll drop to the floor, its emotionless face landing where it could stare at Muldoon. Sarah said nothing for a moment and sat down in a chair, looking drained. "She needs her mother, Inspector. It's hard when she's in the house, but she can't see her."

"It must be, but I'm sure you are doing a fine job," was all he could think to say.

"You're not around little children much, are you?" she said with a smile.

Muldoon smiled back, relaxing his shoulders. "Is it that obvious?"

Sarah laughed, despite herself. "It is. It is."

"Guilty," he said, raising his hands. "They're an anomaly to me."

"To me too, sometimes." She looked back at the dolls and, deciding not to bother tidying, raised her hands and rose out of the chair. "Well, I'll leave you to it. I'll be in the drawing room if you need me. There's no need to visit the park in such foul weather."

He politely moved out of her way as she left the nursery, catching her scent as she passed. It immediately brought his attention back to the other smell: potpourri. Sarah smelled like the room—lavender. He approached the dresser at the far end of the room and lifted the small dish of potpourri to his nose. There was so much of it, in every upstairs room. He looked around at the chaos of the toys that lay strewn across the floor—dolls, bears, clowns and horses. He had never seen so many toys. Finding himself faced with the unwelcome surfacing of a childhood memory, he distracted himself by looking over to where Elsie Bryant slept. Beside the little canopied bed, he spied a music box and went over to it. It opened in the middle of a tune. The hairs on the back of his neck stood erect as his ears processed the familiar melody.

Last night as I lay on my pillow,

Last night as I lay on my bed,

Last night as I lay on my pillow,

I dreamed that my Bon-
nie was dead.

He reflected for a moment and closed the lid of the music box. It was just a song, but he took out his notebook and scribbled a few notes anyway. The rain was still drumming on the window sill outside, accompanied by the occasional crack of thunder. Mrs Bryant was not possessed, but he still didn't have the full story. He closed the book and put it away, sliding the pencil into his breast pocket.

He stood up again and silently walked around the room, opening drawers and trunks. The child, predictably, owned only clothes and toys. The governess had a bible, a stack of books, clothing, shawls and journals. He held back at first, but decided to flick through anyway. He hoped he'd find nothing but musings and entries about long lost lovers, or adventures she hoped to have one day.

"Inspector," Sarah said, leaning into the doorway of the nursery. The journal he was looking at flew out of his hand with a clatter. She couldn't see him in her bedroom from where she was standing, but he felt the awkwardness through the wall. He burst back into the nursery and looked over to where she was standing. "I didn't mean to startle you. It's just that Mrs Mckinnon was going to make some coffee soon and..." she eyed him suspiciously as he brushed an errant tendril of black hair back from his forehead. "We wondered if you would like some when you are finished here?"

"Grand, Miss Jones. That'd be grand. I'm just er..."

His tongue, all of a sudden, seemed too large to facilitate any more words. He looked back into the alcove where Sarah's bed rested under a window, and then back at her. He wanted to say: *I deal with demons, vampires and all the 'weird shit' your type are terribly, terribly frightened of, and a murder investigation isn't usually in my line of work, but I felt sorry for you all and that poor woman downstairs is suffering at the hands of something evil, so here I am rifling through the governess' knicker drawer and feeling embarrassed about it because you're looking at me now with those eyes, Miss Jones,* but his mouth didn't move.

She smiled again with a knowing look. "I understand, Inspector. You have to look." She turned away slowly and went back downstairs.

He returned to the alcove and picked the journal back up. It saddened him that Sarah Jones did not seem to live a wild, secret life where she batted suitors away everywhere she went and wrote about it. He put it back and picked up another, larger one with leather binding. It wasn't a journal but a sketchbook.

Inside were several drawings of hands, faces, animals, objects and people undertaking everyday tasks. He thought they were wonderful as he studied them. He flicked through a few more and stopped when the page fell open at a portrait of Elsie, picking flowers in what he supposed must have been the park or the garden. She had ribbons in her curled hair and smiled as she held a bundle of posies. The way Sarah had drawn her face was so natural, so life-like. The girl in the drawing was a million miles away from the red-faced berserker he had just witnessed fleeing the scene.

To be privy to an artist's intimate drawings filled him with awe, but he also felt he shouldn't enjoy them. Sarah Jones had permitted him to inspect her room, but not her soul. It felt personal—inappropriate, even, to look at her drawings.

This was still an investigation, but he was deeply impressed by the talents of Sarah Jones. Needing one more minute with the book, he turned the page to find a drawing he hadn't expected. Rather than a pencil or charcoal sketch depicting a picturesque scene or everyday people, the image was a man's face. He was handsome, but severe in the way his eyes were fixed on the viewer. The entire background was black, filled in by charcoal. He stood before the shadow, staring. Muldoon, deciding that this picture was the strangest of the collection, pulled it out, folded it, and placed it inside his own notebook. He returned all other items to the chest and closed it carefully.

Remembering that he had said *yes* to coffee, he left the room and gave it one last check from the doorway. The toys were still strewn about the carpet, and the rain hadn't ceased yet, but the nursery seemed changed. He looked over at the large wardrobe that he hadn't explored and went to it quickly. Moving some jackets and dresses out of the way, he jumped when he saw a pair of eyes looking back at him from the dark recesses of the wardrobe. *Get a grip, Muldoon,* he thought as he picked up a little doll that had been left sitting there. "What are you doing here?" he asked, looking at the doll. He turned away from the wardrobe and thought of where he could place it. He settled it down on the child's bed and finally left the room.

Passing the master bedroom on his way down, he decided to knock. There was no answer, so he stepped back and turned to face the staircase. He was halted in his tracks when he heard it swing open behind him.

Almost filling the width of the doorway was Dr Swinson, the man he had met half an hour before. "Hello, doctor," Muldoon said. "I wondered if—"

Swinson shook his head. "You can try, my lad, but I'm afraid she will just babble now."

Muldoon raised an eyebrow. Swinson continued talking, "Mrs Bryant is—well put it this way—" his red face was sweating slightly, glistening in the dim light, "it is a privilege for her not to have to go to the asylum."

"I see," he said, revealing nothing. The doctor stepped out onto the landing and closed the bedroom door.

"I'm afraid there is not much that can be done for her, now," he said gravely.

"I'm very sorry to hear that, doctor."

"Aye. It is a shame." Swinson bowed his head and gestured toward the stairs. "I'll follow you down." Muldoon turned and descended the stairs, waiting for the doctor to join him in the hallway. "So, you're a private investigator?"

"I'm a Detective Inspector, doctor."

Swinson looked him up and down, taking into account the wool suit that the Irishman wore. "If you don't mind me asking... Who do you work for?" he asked after a few heavy breaths through his mouth.

Muldoon reached into his jacket pocket and presented his badge to the doctor, who acknowledged it with a grunt. "I was hoping to catch you today, actually," Muldoon said, studying the older man's face. Dr Swinson seemed preoccupied, looking to the front door and back.

"I do have to get back," Swinson said, looking at his watch. He caught Muldoon's stare and shrugged, "but I suppose I could spare you five minutes."

"Thank you, doctor. When were you first called to visit Mrs Bryant?"

"Oh," Swinson said, scratching his head. "It was a while ago. Some time during the summer when Mr Bryant was still around. She'd been having hallucinations, he said."

"What kind of hallucinations, doctor?"

"I seem to remember the husband saying something about blood..." Swinson looked around the hallway and continued, "blood coming from the walls. The ceiling, that sort of thing." Muldoon nodded, listening encouragingly. "Nasty stuff, but that's hysteria for you."

Muldoon nodded again and asked, "had Mrs Bryant had any history of hallucinations?"

He shook his head firmly, his face wobbling like a presentation of jelly that Muldoon had seen at a party once. "I'm afraid I don't really know the Bryant's too well, Inspector..." he looked around again and lowered his voice, "but between you and me, the woman is mad. Driven to it or born that way—she's as mad as a box of frogs if you'll excuse the expression. We caught her hiding a razor. She hasn't harmed anyone, but if you ask me, that woman belongs in the asylum."

Muldoon thought for a moment. "Why is she not there, if that's your diagnosis, doctor?"

He turned his bulbous nose upward. "The family have the money to keep her at home. It's as simple as that." He walked over to the coat stand and reached for his hat, cane and jacket. "Now, if you'll excuse me Inspector..."

"Muldoon, doctor."

"Inspector Muldoon. I have appointments all afternoon."

The doctor struggled to get his coat back on; Muldoon judged that it had recently become a size too small and the old man was still in the frustrating period of denial. He placed his hands in his pockets and said, "of course, doctor. Thank you for your time." Muldoon thought about the ghost's bloodied neck and raised a hand. "Just one more thing, doctor. Where can I find this razor?"

Swinson frowned. "What would you want that for?"

"The investigation, doctor. It may help with—"

"I'm afraid I don't know, Inspector," Swinson said haughtily. "Ask the mother. Goodbye."

Swinson saw himself out, casting another look back at the inspector before tipping his hat and leaving. Muldoon stood still for a moment, thinking about the words that had just been exchanged. The woman he had spoken to didn't seem mad, but he was no doctor. Something about Swinson made him question the doctor's statement. He turned on his heel to go and see Frances for himself but just as he did, Mrs Mckinnon came marching out of the passage leading to the kitchen. "Ah! Inspector," she said. "There's coffee in the kitchen if you would like some?"

"Thank you, Mrs Mckinnon. I'll be there in a moment."

He silently raced up the stairs, skipping two steps at a time. When he reached the door of Frances' room, he hesitated for a moment, thinking of what he wanted to know. Finally, he opened the door after gently knocking and stepped in.

Frances didn't seem to have moved from the position she was in when he last saw her. His heart sank. She was staring at the ceiling, but the life in her face had depleted further. Her ghastly visage reminded him of a waxwork, devoid of natural life and hardly blinking. The woman in the photograph was no more, at least, not at that moment. "Frances," Muldoon said quietly. She didn't seem to register his voice. "Frances, I wondered if we could finish that conversation?" She didn't answer. He looked around the bed and noticed that the tray of bottles was gone; only a glass of water stood on the bedside table.

He leaned over and looked into her eyes. The pupils were constricted. Stepping back, he brought his hand to his chin and thought about his next move. The room was well-lit, but only by candles and gas lamps. He blew out a couple of candles and dimmed the lamps, returning to Frances. Her pupils remained narrow. He crossed the room and forcibly threw the heavy curtains open. A groan came from deep within the throat of the catatonic Frances, but he saw that she couldn't turn her head away from the grey light outside as it bounced off the mirrors and into her face. The sun wasn't shining as much as he'd have liked, but he had to be sure. He gently felt the muscles in her face; they were as set as a plaster mask.

Muldoon returned to the kitchen and crossed paths with Sarah once more. She cast her eyes downward as she left the room, "Inspector," she said with the tiniest bow.

Mrs Mckinnon had been clearing away some cups, and put them in the sink so she could make space and pour out some coffee for the inspector. He sat down in the small wooden chair at the head of the table and watched the steaming brown liquid fall into his cup like a silk ribbon.

"Thank you. I am sorry that I was later than planned."

Mrs Mckinnon issued him with her charming , worldly-wise smile. "Say no more of it, Inspector. We're glad to have you here."

There was an authenticity to the housekeeper's tone, and she didn't hide her feelings like other women liked to do. "I've a lot to go on, Mrs Mckinnon," he said, "but this is going to take some time, I think." He thought of the elusive Margaret Ross and her letters, the blubbering Mrs Larkin, the shifty doctor Swinson, the tear that Mrs Bryant had shed when they parted, and the way Sarah had looked at him when she returned to the nursery. Were they all hiding something from him, or was there only one of them hiding in the crowd? He sipped his coffee while he pondered. "I shall have to report back to my superiors and return to you some time later this week."

"Very well," Mrs Mckinnon said. "I'll let Mrs Larkin know." She left him to drink his coffee in silence.

21

"Well, what have you found then?" Gill asked, sitting down in his chair for once.

Muldoon sighed and lit a cigarette. "Too much. God, Gov, why did it have to be me?"

Gill flashed him a mischievous smile. "Weird shit, then?"

Muldoon's long black eyelashes outlined his bloodshot eyes like a lead window frame. He rubbed them, furthering the discomfort. Everywhere he looked, there was something to be suspicious of, but he couldn't use everything as a lead at the same time. He thought of Frances Bryant's deathly pallor and the endless blubbering of Beatrice Larkin. He felt heavy in his chair. "You could say that," he said. "It's a house full of women and one of them appears to be mad."

"All women are mad, Daniel. Psychosis on legs—the lot of them. Mad, bad or sad."

Muldoon flicked some ash into the ceramic ashtray and smirked. "How's Mrs Gill?"

"Sad," Gill said, blowing smoke out of his nostrils, "because I'm in here with these hapless bastards all night. The only difference between me and them is I'm getting paid for it—and they're scum, I suppose." He leaned back in the chair and crossed his legs, nursing a glass of scotch in his hands. "So, is there a ghost or what?" he said, his pipe bobbing up and down with the movement of his mouth.

"There's a ghost all right." Muldoon took a deep drag of his cigarette and exhaled slowly, thinking. He couldn't recall a time when he had smoked as much as he had in the last two days, and studied his cigarette case, thinking about the woman in the box.

"Haunting *you* by the looks of it." Gill was more open-minded when he'd had a drink. He put his scotch back on the desk and held his pipe, sucking the life out of it. The amber glow caught his eye as he prepared his answer.

"There's more than one ghost," Muldoon said with a sigh.

"Yeah? Christ." Gill shuddered. "Who better to handle it though, eh?"

"I managed to catch the doctor today. Had to flash him this badge you made me."

"Really?"

"This is the thing, Gill, and it did make me wonder..." Muldoon leaned in over the desk to look at him closely. "Why are we still working together? Why am I still parading around with this badge? I'm not a real police officer. Why am I here?"

"Because I need you."

"That's all?"

"You saved my life, Muldoon," Gill said gravely. "You saved my family."

Muldoon tried to speak but Gill spoke louder. "That was the first time—and this is the honest to God truth—the first time I ever, ever feared for my life as a police officer." Gill scrunched his face up for a moment and continued. "This city's evil, Mulders. It's not just the gangs and the thieves and the corrupt factory owners—something grows here, like a fucking fungus. Down the sewers or something—I don't know, but you get my point. Since this place started filling up with people fifty years ago, it's rotten. It stinks." Muldoon raised an eyebrow. "No, not 'cos of the Irish. Piss off with your victim card. You know what I mean. There's evil everywhere and I've never met anyone like you. You just handle it like it's normal. I need you on my team, Mulders. It's dark out there. Even if you are a strange bastard. There's always something kicking off in the underworld. The *real* underworld, and I can't do it alone. It scares me shitless. If people knew the truth, they wouldn't sleep at night."

Muldoon looked down at his lap and grinned. "I'd agree with that," he said dryly.

Silence edged its way in and sat between them for a few moments while they smoked together. Gill, returning from a deep thought, put his pipe down and folded his arms. "So what's next then?" he asked. Where's the husband?"

"Definitely not at home. The housekeeper says he's in South Africa. I don't know much about him other than that he struck gold a few years ago and now he's doing something similar down there, scrapping over land with Zulus or the Dutch or something."

"You might find this of interest, then," Gill said, opening a drawer in his desk and lifting out an envelope. "Deeds to number five, Percy Street. It says that Mr John Bryant has been the owner of that house for ten years. Let's hope the ghost has been around longer than he has, or we're looking for a body."

Muldoon flicked through the images of the day in his mind. "You think there's been a murder?" he asked, knowing full well that Mary had tried to speak to tell him about it.

"It'd be good if there 'ad. I've got a toff's missing persons list as long as the road to bloody Wigan Pier and back." Muldoon's mouth dangled open in disbelief. "Yeah," Gill continued. "Kidnaps, murders, suicides. Those rich bastards are messed up in the head. Had two brothers kill each other last week in a shoot up over inheritance. Twins."

Muldoon, grateful to not have had too many dealings with regular policing, shook his head. "There's a ghost I've seen, sir, but I don't know if it's connected to the Bryants' yet." He shrugged. "It's not your classic haunted house or family curse type of thing. They're new money."

Gill put his pipe down, stood up and stretched. "So? Money's money. They have a lot of it. I wouldn't put it past them. Rich killer, poor killer—everybody shits, Mulders." Muldoon, interrupted by a passing thought, wondered about the mysterious Mr Ellman for a moment.

"Are any women on the missing list called Mary?"

Gill stared at him incredulously. "Are you having a laugh? Mary, Margaret, Sarah. They're all called one of those names. You'll have to narrow it down somewhat."

"How will I do that?"

"You'll have to ask one of the sergeants downstairs to find that out. How old does she look? The ghost, like?"

"Hard to tell. She's dead. All dead people look ageless, and at the same time old and decrepit."

Gill shrank away in disgust and picked up his pipe again. "Well, when you find out, you get your lucky Irish arse over here and we'll bring the squad."

"I'll have one more sweep of the house tomorrow and then I'll have to go wider. I'll speak to the employer. He might be able to tell me something about Bryant."

Muldoon stubbed his cigarette out and reached for his coat. Gill walked over to the door to let him out but he could see that the Chief Inspector was thinking deeply about something he'd rather not have been.

"Goodnight, sir."

"Night, Mulders."

Muldoon stopped in his shadowed doorway beneath the coos of nesting pigeons and turned the key in the front door. Stepping into his dark office, he dumped his coat and keys onto the table and reached for his matches to light a lamp. It was at that moment that he heard the sound of two people clambering down the stairs that connected him to Mae Magnusson's premises. "I told you he'd be back, love," he heard Mae saying to someone else. Their shoes clacked heavily on the rough wood steps, echoing down the hallway.

He approached the connecting door and unlocked it just as Mae rapped her bejewelled knuckles on the wood. She jumped back at the sudden opening of the door. "Oh, there you are," she said, smiling with her rouged lips. Her wig for the evening was an unnatural red, and he noticed she had acquired a beauty spot on her cheek overnight.

"Everything all right, Mae?" he asked. Mae turned her head to look back to the stairs, where someone was still coming down. It was Sarah Jones, looking more uncomfortable than he had ever seen her before.

"This pretty little thing came looking for you. Says she knows you." Mae winked. "I said I bet she does."

"Miss Jones," Muldoon said, alarmed by her presence in the corridor. Sarah's cheeks flushed crimson, contrasting with her bright green eyes.

"She came in through our door. But don't worry, we were very hospitable, weren't we darlin'?"

"Yes, very much so." Sarah's lips slammed together to create something halfway between nervously smiling and cringing.

"Right, I'll leave you to it," Mae said with a cheeky smile. "I've got a business to run." The older woman giggled and almost ran back up the stairs, leaving Sarah and the inspector in the corridor. The sound of loud, jaunty piano music and laughter floated down the stairs until they heard her close the door with a slam.

"You could have told me you lived in a bawdy house," Sarah said, almost under her breath.

"I don't?" he said, taken aback. "Why were you up there?"

Sarah pulled two cards out of her pocket and presented them to him. "This one is the card you gave me, and this one is one I found in the house. It's the same building, is it not?"

"I'm a tenant, yes. I'm 10a though, as you can see here." He pointed to the address at the bottom of the card he had given her. She blinked with embarrassment.

"At a glance, they looked the same. I walked in through the street entrance and—I shall probably never live it down."

He smiled, finding himself pleased to have company. "No one will have seen you. Anyway, did you want to come in?"

Sarah followed him into his office and waited in the dark while he flitted about the room lighting the lamps. When she could see it, she sat down on the tattered armchair in the corner. She looked about the modest room and spied an open door at the back, where a single, brass bed rested on a long-neglected brick wall, adorned only by a wooden crucifix.

Muldoon awkwardly approached a small table in the corner where a single bottle of scotch stood and asked, "would you like one?"

"I think I need one, don't you?" she asked. They both laughed.

"The girls are all right. Mae is a good landlady. Never gives me any trouble." He brought Sarah a glass of scotch. She thanked him and held it in her hands. "So what can I do for you, Miss Jones?"

"You said I should contact you if I had anything that would help and... I think *this* might." She retrieved the card again and held it out to him. He took it gently and read the scrawl on the back.

"It's a calling card. Where did you find it?"

"In the wardrobe. I was putting some of Elsie's things away and it was there, on the bottom. I thought it might have been yours." She watched him take a sip of his drink and shake his head. He looked at her for a moment, thinking.

Sarah straightened in the chair. "Well it's not mine!"

"I know how it looks, but I assure you I haven't seen Madame Chloe. I don't *see* anyone upstairs—"

"It's none of my business if you do."

"Now, look—"

"No, please. I just thought it might be yours or... someone might have left it."

"Correct me if I'm wrong but, it's a house full of women, Miss Jones."

"That's why it's strange, isn't it?"

"Well, yes..." He didn't see the card when he had been there that day. "I suppose you're right."

"So what are you going to do?"

"Well, I don't know yet," he said, deepening the creases at the corner of each eye with his smile. "What do you think I should do?"

"I don't know." She slapped a hand down on her lap. "Now I feel silly."

He sat down in the wooden chair opposite. "There's no need to feel silly. You brought me something that you thought would be useful, and it might be!"

"Do you think so?"

"Perhaps it belonged to Mr Bryant?"

Her eyes widened in horror. "Mr Bryant? No, that's not possible."

"He's been away for a time—"

"No!" Sarah's eyes were beautiful when indignant, and they were burning through his face. "Mr Bryant and Frances—they love each other. I mean, it's like they're not married at all the way they are with one another," she cast her eyes downward, "if you catch my meaning."

"Men don't seek the services of whores because they don't love their wives, Miss Jones," Muldoon began, "it's perfectly normal for sailors, for example—"

"No." She shook her head vehemently. "Please don't patronise me, Inspector. It's not like that." Her eyes twinkled with the impending swell of tears. "It's the thing you read about in storybooks." She scoffed and shook her head. "You may think me a naive woman, but I know things can go on behind closed doors between families. I assure you, Mr Bryant wouldn't do that."

Muldoon was stunned by her passionate statement. "You said to me earlier that you barely know the man, Miss Jones."

"True," she said as she nodded, "but I know Frances. If he was interested in other women, she would know. I can only measure his character by what he means to her, and it's not something he would do to her."

"How can you be so sure?"

"I can't. It's just a feeling. But by all means, go on and think what you like. They are just my thoughts, really. Besides, he's been out of the country for nearly three months. Why would this card appear now?"

Muldoon enjoyed her inquisitiveness, and gave an approving nod. "Perhaps someone wanted us to find it."

"Are you going to ask this... *Madame Chloe* about him?" Her lips curved into a sneer as she said the words *Madame Chloe*. He found it quite amusing.

"I might. Do you want to come with me?" he asked, raising his eyebrows.

"Heavens, no!"

Muldoon laughed. "I'm just teasing, Miss Jones. I can ask her another time."

Sarah studied him for a moment. The fire of the whiskey spread through her chest, easing the tension in her body as her muscles relaxed into the chair. There was no fire lit in the room, but she felt warm. Her eyes began to relax.

"Do you know who called for the doctor, Miss Jones?"

The question stirred her from her apparent drowsiness as she processed it. "I don't know," she said, cocking her head. "I thought it might have been Beatrice, but I don't know."

"Perhaps it was." He stuck out his chin while he was thinking of his next question. "What do you think of the doctor?"

"I don't really know. I haven't thought about him," she said, resting her chin on her hand. "He's just a doctor. Talks too much, and Frances can't stand him, but he..." she trailed off, as though someone had interrupted her thoughts. "He hasn't said what he's doing or why... I suppose. I mean, I'm just the governess, but Beatrice has nobody else to talk to."

"Do you know what the medicine is that he's prescribing?"

She shook her head. "I haven't been in her room for a while. I've only been asked to sit with her once or twice. My duty is to Elsie."

"Of course it is," he agreed. "What exactly, in your eyes, is wrong with your mistress?"

Sarah leaned forward. "Something happened, after the seance," she began, "the house hasn't been the same since, and neither has she. It's like... that ouija board gave life to something. Things move around, and I know I haven't touched them, nor have I seen anyone in the room. As far as I know, the maid cleans the nursery once a week but it's myself and Elsie in there most of the time. When you live with children, you know when a child has touched something. There will be grease marks or sticky fingerprints, or of course, they knock it over and don't pick it up. I myself have never really believed in ghosts, and I wasn't sure if Frances did, either, but something speaks to her. I fear that she has no choice but to listen." She sipped some more whiskey. "I don't know if it torments her..." she looked directly into his eyes, "or if it has become her."

He loosened the collar of his shirt. Hours before, the ghost of Mary had grabbed it, and tried to pull him into a chest. "Can you tell me what the others think?"

"Her mother seems to think that she is possessed. I think Mrs Larkin is fearful, and weeps as though Frances has died already. Of course, Beatrice was in that room with them when it happened—the seance, that is—and she has not uttered a word about it since. I think she feels rather guilty—the seance being her idea—and is having trouble dealing with it, which is understandable."

"And the other members of the seance?"

"Oh," Sarah bit her bottom lip in thought. Muldoon waited, crossing his legs and listening carefully. "The medium is called Mr Kingsley, and he brought with him another man—Fred. I'm sorry..." She lowered her shoulders and frowned. "I can't for the life of me remember his surname."

"That's all right. I'll arrange a meeting with them, if I have an address?"

"I'm sure you could. Beatrice has their address."

"Thank you, Miss Jones. Back to the ghosts, then—and give me the first answer you have. Do you think that the house is haunted or not?" Muldoon, even if he knew the truth, still liked to know the opinions of occupants. Their usual inability to see or hear ghosts fascinated him.

Sarah pulled her shawl tightly over her shoulders and rubbed her arms. "It could be. That's the only way to explain what's happened, surely."

"Does anything strange happen in the nursery, or your room?"

"I can't say I've noticed. It's a little cold in there, sometimes, but that's to be expected." She covered a yawn and sipped some more of her drink. Muldoon lifted his glass to her and asked if she wanted another. She shook her head.

"It's quite late, Inspector Muldoon. I should think about going home."

"I'll walk you."

"Thank you, I would like that."

They strolled uphill through the lamp-lit streets that glistened with the damp of the autumn evening until they reached St Bride's church on the corner. The white facets of the unusual building stood out against the dim brickwork of its surroundings, like a temple on a mount. Sarah, flushed from the exertion, stopped for a moment to adjust her shoe when Muldoon stopped and looked around cautiously. They were surrounded only by the spotlights of the gas lamps and the shadowy buildings, but he sensed they were being watched. He held a finger to his mouth. They both listened. The shrubs in the churchyard beside them rustled. Sarah instinctively positioned herself behind the inspector and squinted into the darkness.

"Dooney!"

It was Paulie, leaping over the wall of the churchyard, excited to see the inspector. Sarah sighed with relief, holding her hand on her chest. "Paulie!" Muldoon called, "what are you doing in there?"

"I was followin' ye, but I wasn't sure if it was you."

"Why?"

Paulie looked up at them with large, bashful eyes. "You've got a lady with ye."

Sarah blushed. "How long have you been following us?" Muldoon asked.

"I was outside yours and followed you up. Mae said you were busy with a lady and tha' I shouldn' bother ye, so I waited on the corner. Ye didn't see me tho' did ye?" The boy grinned and stuck his chest out.

Muldoon laughed. "No, Paulie. You're a fine spy."

"I followed that doctor like ye asked." He produced a diary and handed it to the inspector, who took it gratefully.

"Paulie, I only asked for reconnaissance."

"Re-con-eh-wa?" The boy scrunched his filthy face up in bewilderment. Sarah laughed.

"Reconnaissance, Paulie. It's French, I think."

"Don't know no French," the boy said, kicking at some leaves with tatty boots that were only half-laced.

"Well, thank you anyway. You really didn't have to, and I wasn't supposed to be meeting with you 'til next week. Why are you out so late?"

"Me da's got a new woman. Doesn't want me in tonight."

Sarah blinked with an open mouth, wondering if she'd heard right. Muldoon, knowing exactly what she was thinking, gave her a regretful nod.

"Paulie, you need somewhere else to stay," Muldoon said, reaching inside his jacket for some money. The boy shrugged.

"Nah, he'll let me back in at er, what time is it?"

Muldoon checked his watch. "Ten o'clock."

"He'll let me back in at five when he gets up for work. It's only a few hours."

If it was possible for a heart to shatter, Sarah's was about to crack. She didn't know what to say, and thought of her own warm bed waiting for her with a pang of guilt. Elsie Bryant, not much younger than the urchin, slept only a few houses away, safe in the knowledge that she had a roof over her head.

"Could we at least give you some tea, Paulie?" Sarah suggested, looking back to Muldoon for what—approval? She wasn't sure what the nature of their relationship was. "I live just there," she said, pointing to the row of houses opposite the church. "I'm sure my mistress wouldn't mind."

"That's very kind of you, Miss Jones, but I'll take him back with me. I'm sure Mae will need someone to give her a hand digging fallen coins out of the floorboards, or cleaning the grate or something. Let us walk you home."

The boy bumbled along behind them as they walked to number five. He waited at the front gate while Muldoon accompanied Sarah to the doorstep. Across the number on the door, a large spider was weaving a web in the lamplight between the knocker and the column beside it, just in time to catch any unsuspecting passers-by. "I feel terrible when I have to walk through a web," Sarah said, wincing.

"Allow me." Muldoon picked up a stick and gathered the web, relocating both web and spider to another corner of the porch. She smiled and thanked him. "Thank you for your help this evening," Muldoon said. Sarah unlocked the door and went inside, temporarily illuminating Muldoon and the garden path before everything returned to darkness once more.

"Is that your sweetheart then?" Paulie asked as Muldoon closed the gate behind him.

Muldoon laughed and ruffled the boy's mop of black hair as they walked back down the hill towards the river. "You're not on duty now, Paulie. Button it."

22

HAVING FAILED TO CONVINCE Mae that Paulie could help around her premises, Muldoon instead offered Paulie a bed in his dwelling. Mae agreed to bring down a mattress for him to sleep on, and as it was cold down there, she also provided an extra blanket. "Upstairs is no place for children, Daniel," she insisted.

"There's nowhere he can go where he won't see anything?"

"It's been a while since you've been to this kind of place, hasn't it?" she said, rolling her heavy brown eyes. "I'll not have children in here. I had a girl last week insisting she was old enough. Said it must have been easier than selling matches on the street. I sent her away. Said she could clean for me if she was desperate, but I won't have it. Life's short enough." She made the sign of the cross and adjusted her shawl.

Muldoon held his hands up in surrender. "I hadn't thought it through, Mae."

She pulled a blanket from the store room cupboard. "You don't say." She handed it to him and assessed her dishevelled tenant. "Who's the girl then?"

"Miss Jones? She's part of the investigation."

"Didn't look like that to me."

"It never does, Mae." He turned to walk away.

"She's rather helpful, coming all the way out here to speak to you."

"That she is." Muldoon opened the door and stepped out into the hallway. "Thank you, Mae."

Muldoon lay wide awake in his bed. Paulie, on the other hand, had fallen asleep within minutes of receiving the mattress. The small boy slept curled up like a dog in front of Muldoon's meagre fire, his blanket up to his chin. The little boots that he had bought with his wages rested by the back door. At first, Muldoon was distracted by the boy's gentle snoring, but after some time, it settled into the natural rhythm of the basement.

He chuckled to himself when he heard an abrupt fart echo across the adjoining rooms. He hadn't had a housemate for a long time, or even a pet for that matter.

He'd brought his case file into his bedroom with him with the intention of reviewing his findings in bed, but he was pre-occupied by the doctor's diary that sat on his bedside table. Frustratingly, Swinson wrote in code, and Muldoon was too tired to decipher it. It taunted him silently, daring him to open it and try again. Muldoon, unable to face it, rolled over and tried to get some sleep.

His dreams were vivid that night. He dreamt that he was sitting on a park bench with Sarah. They watched Elsie play with a kite on the hill overlooking the river. Swans sailed across the pond behind her, and it was a clear, windy day. He turned to look at Sarah, who was wearing a white cotton gown—the one he'd seen on the dressmaker's dummy in the guest room of Percy Street. She looked beautiful, with loose wavy hair hanging down to her waist.

"Well done, Elsie," she said, as Elsie effortlessly flew the kite. Sarah's sketchbook lay open on the floor at their feet, and Muldoon bent down to pick it up. Placing it on his lap, he admired the drawing that Sarah had done of Elsie flying a kite. The wind flicked past another handful of pages and opened again at the ghastly image of the man staring at him. He turned to look at Sarah and saw that she was furious. "How dare you," she said, slapping him across the face.

"Who is he? Who is he, Sarah?" Muldoon asked, surprising even himself with the amount of emotion in his voice. "What does he mean to you?"

He stole one more look at the dark stranger glaring at him from the paper before she picked up the book and walked away, asking Elsie to follow. Elsie let go of the kite and ran to her governess, holding her hand and turning to look once more at Muldoon. He looked on in bewilderment as Elsie placed a finger to her lips and said "shh."

They were standing on the hill looking down at him—three of them: Mary, Elsie and Sarah. Elsie stood between them, holding their hands. Muldoon rose from the bench and fixed his attention on Mary, who wasn't bleeding any more, nor was she difficult to look at. Her face was clean, and there was no gash on her neck. She smiled down at Elsie, who smiled back. Lying between Muldoon and the women on the hill, was a line of dolls.

Muldoon woke to see that the room was still pitch black. He wondered if he'd even been asleep, and rolled over to check his pocket watch. It was midnight. From the other room, he could hear Paulie babbling in his sleep and smacking his lips together. He reached for his matches and struck one, lighting the gas lamp beside his bed.

Fumbling through the case file, he pulled out his evidence and looked over it, starting with Frances' letters.

> Please come home. I don't give a damn about Mr
> Ellman–I need you here with me. Tell me where
> he is and I shall go to him myself. He has no right
> to keep you from me.

He chewed on the name for a time and fell asleep.

Some time after he had drifted off, he woke again. From the way the room was lit in pale grey, he estimated that it must have been dawn. Muldoon cleared the grit from his eyes, yawned, and checked his pocket watch. It was nearly five o'clock in the morning. Gulls screeched outside at the docks, and he heard the faint clip-clopping of hooves somewhere out on the street. He closed his eyes for a moment, and thought of the strange dream.

Unable to drift off again, he stared at the ceiling for a few minutes before the urge to use his chamber pot prevented him from relaxing any further. He got up and completed his usual morning routine, shaving the stubble from his face. As the razor glided up his neck, gently sliding across his adam's apple, he thought of Mary's ghost and her gaping throat. The distraction made him flinch; he caught a small trickle of blood rolling down his neck in the tiny shaving mirror. He picked up a towel and tended to it, thinking of the razor that Frances had. He went back to his case file and looked through the stack of letters again, searching for one in particular.

> Anyway, I climbed to the attic. Mary showed me the way. I slipped into the entrance. It was so dark, but the potpourri was comforting and I slid the panel with ease. The little staircase is rather cold, but the room remains usable. There she was, on her hands and knees, looking right at me. Early morning light was trying its best to shine through the bricked up windows... She cannot speak, what with her throat being cut but she can

touch things and move things. She lifted the lid

of a chest beside her and passed me a razor.

Muldoon sank down onto the bed and stared at the letter once more. *Potpourri*. He recalled Sarah's description of the nursery: "it's a little cold in there, sometimes." His stomach churned with excitement when he remembered the doll, staring at him. *Mary needs her maids in a row!*

"Paulie!" he called. "Paulie, wake up!"

The little lad rolled over and groaned. "What time is it?"

"Dolls in a row, Paulie—no, maids! Mary, er, something about a garden. Paulie, is there a song, or a story or something? A pretty garden and a row of maids?"

The boy sat up and rubbed his eyes. "It's a girl song... Mary, Mary..." he hummed the rest until he got to "and pretty maids all in a row."

"Paulie, you genius!" Muldoon clapped his hands together and paced the room in thought. "It's too early—but I'll get you some bread and bacon and I've got to get to the bridewell. I'll leave you with some breakfast and you do—do whatever, sleep in, whatever. Go home if you like." He went back to his room to finish dressing. "Hang on," he said, speaking to nobody in particular. "Gill was on the night shift, which means he's still there. Right, here's some money. Go and get yourself something to eat when you wake up." He came back into his office and slammed the spare key down along with a few coins before returning to his room. He secured the knot in his tie and bustled out of his office with his case file and jacket in his arms, leaving Paulie to drift back off to sleep again.

Gill was just about to leave when Muldoon came bursting into the bridewell foyer. "It'd better be good, Mulders. I was looking forward to a hot breakfast," Gill said, adjusting his jacket.

"I think I know where the body is."

Gill, Muldoon and a bleary-eyed Constable Lacey were the first to arrive at Percy street where they met three other constables at the door of the house. Muldoon stepped back from the house and looked at it, then he turned his head to observe the neighbouring properties. "Look," he said to Gill, pointing at number five. "Every house on this street has windows at the top except for this one."

"And?" asked Gill, half asleep and fully irritated.

"They're attic windows. They've been bricked up."

"Well what are we waiting for, then?" Gill asked.

"Just let me get up there and warn them. They're probably still asleep."

After a yawning Mrs Mckinnon let him in, Muldoon went in first and headed straight to the nursery. Sarah was still in her nightgown when he knocked. He averted his eyes from the thin cotton gown she wore at the door of the nursery. "Miss Jones, we need to come into the nursery. Could you wake the child and evacuate the premises, please?"

Her long plait of hair hung down her left breast and she covered the right with her arm. "Do I have time to dress?"

Muldoon checked his watch. "Be as quick as you can. There are a lot of anxious policemen waiting outside. Myself included." Her lips parted to say something but she stopped herself and closed the door. He heard her rush around the room, gently rousing Elsie. Five minutes later, they came out of the room. Sarah, now fully dressed, held a sleepy Elsie in her arms—the little girl's chin resting on her shoulder. "Here," he said, lifting Elsie out of her arms. "I've got to lock you up in the drawing room."

Sarah went ahead of him down the stairs without question. He carried Elsie down and placed her on the sofa of the drawing room. "Please don't come out. Don't let her see anything," he said before leaving the room.

Muldoon ran back up the stairs, puffing and panting until he was back in the nursery. From the window of the nursery, he waved a hand and gestured for Gill to follow him up.

Muldoon, the bile rising in his throat, stepped over to the wardrobe and opened it. He put his hand inside, heading for the back; he found a bag of potpourri dangling from a hook. He grabbed it and pulled it out. Annoyed with himself for missing it the first time, he tossed the bag of lavender aside and reached in again. He banged on the panel at the back of the wardrobe. Nothing. Using both hands, he gave the back panel a shove. Nothing. Running his fingers up the corners of the panel, he noticed that there was a small gap between the side of the panel and the side of the wardrobe. Sticking his finger into the gap, he nudged it to the left. The panel slid across like a door. His heart leapt into his throat.

"What is it, sir?" asked a constable behind him. It was Lacey.

Muldoon pulled his head out of the wardrobe and with a flash of intensity in his eyes, he grinned. "It's the jackpot, Lacey."

Lacey peered in behind Muldoon as he climbed back into the wardrobe and completely opened the panel. "Lacey, remove these things from the wardrobe and follow me up," he said, feeling for the first step of the staircase in front of him.

Constable Lacey hurried to remove the clothes and laid them on the small bed. He hesitated for a moment when he was faced with the entrance, as something made his nose curl.

"Lacey, get up here, and bring a crowbar," Muldoon called, "and be quick about it."

The young constable did as he was told, and after acquiring a selection of tools from the outhouse, followed the inspector into the attic.

Part III

23

January 18th, 1886

Dear Margaret,

I know that this letter will cause you pain to read, but you must understand that I am happy. Love can change a man, and I believe that we are in love, and that the pain he caused was nothing more than a young boy's boorishness. What cold hearts they have before they know love!

I would not expect you to see his charming nature, as siblings often cannot, but I assure you that he is kind. He tries to be kind.

Forgive me for leaving as I did, but nobody would have approved. They don't understand him like I do.

Our love is like those we have read about in our books, and you know which one I speak of: "He's more myself than I am. Whatever our souls are made of, his and mine are the same." We are as doomed as we are destined, and I must take my place by his side, for he cannot be without me.

Please tell my mother and father that I am well. It breaks my heart for us to have parted like this, but it is for the best.

I believe in redemption, as I know you do also. We are to go to Europe for our honeymoon. He has promised to take me to Rome.

I hope that we can be friends again, for I love you and Sissy like sisters.

All my love,

Mary

"PUT A WARRANT OUT for Mr Bryant," Gill said, slamming a police file down on Constable Lacey's desk. Young Constable Lacey, true to the form of a broken-in horse, nodded, and headed to the door with his helmet under his arm. "And Lacey, come straight back!"

"Lacey, wait!" called Muldoon, looking at Gill. The gangly, red-faced constable stopped and waited for further orders. "He's already on the ship home. He must be. Shouldn't we keep it quiet so that he gets off the ship?"

Gill stroked his chin. "Good point. Is it stopping off anywhere?"

"I don't know, but let's not take the risk. Let him come home thinking everything's fine."

Gill nodded. "Lacey, just get the signature. No telegraphs. Right—go!" Lacey left the room.

Gill watched Muldoon walk to the window and stand in front of it with his arms folded. "What are you so mopey about? We've got a body."

"We don't know who it is, though."

"No, that's true. You can go back to the house and find out."

Muldoon looked up at the ceiling. "I can't get any sense out of Mrs Bryant," he said regretfully.

"What's wrong with her?"

"I think she's taking opium."

"Well take it off her then!"

Muldoon looked at Gill and held out his hands. "She'll die if I do that."

"Well, find a way, Mulders. Do some of your God magic, I don't know." Gill turned on his heel and headed for the door. "And go and see the employer as well. I want a statement regarding Bryant's character. I'll see if I can get you a doctor. Chop chop!" Gill clapped his hands and pushed his body against the door, opening it with his backside and rolling away. He disappeared down the corridor.

Given the choice between returning to Mrs Bryant or meeting with Mr Bryant's employer, Muldoon decided to try the offices of Ellman and Co. first. Discovering that Ellman was 'at home today,' and having been given the home address of the shipping tycoon by a very helpful young lady secretary, he hopped on a quiet train in the light drizzle to Allerton. Watching the world hurtle past as he sat still in the rocking carriage, Muldoon thought of what he was going to say. As far as he knew, Bryant had worked for Ellman for less than a year, but Ellman appeared to have great influence over the self-made businessman, and something else was particularly interesting to him: the address of Thomas Ellman was the same correspondence address he had seen on the top of Margaret Ross' letters. He felt in his pocket for his badge and relaxed.

The rain had dissipated by the time he reached the house. The mansion in question was an enormous sandstone building, styled in the fashionable 'new gothic' that many properties in the area had adopted. The trees, blazen with orange and red foliage, looked striking against their dark trunks and branches. Shells of conkers and dry, crisp leaves crunched under his boots as he approached Springheath Hall.

He waited at the wrought iron gates for the gatekeeper to come out. When the old man finally materialised, he needed only to take one look at Muldoon's badge and opened the gate, tipping his cap as he closed it behind the visitor. "Mornin' sir."

Muldoon walked up to the great house's steps and waited on the top of them, ringing the bell. A middle-aged maid answered. "I'm here to see Mr Ellman," he said, flashing his badge once more. "I'm Detective Inspector Muldoon." She opened the great door and let him in.

"I'll let him know. Please wait here," she said, scurrying across the impeccably polished floor of the hallway. He removed his hat and waited, looking up at the gilded-framed portraits and paintings along the walls, some of which were taller than the tallest man he knew. A couple of minutes passed before the maid came back. "This way, please."

He followed her over to a sunroom at the back of the house, where an older man was sitting at a table, reading a newspaper in his smoking jacket. He folded the paper and rose from the seat, holding out a hand to Muldoon. "Inspector, what can I do for you today?"

Muldoon shook Ellman's hand firmly. "Mr Ellman, I am here to collect a statement from you."

Ellman gestured for Muldoon to join him in his corner of the room among parlour palms and a decorative bird cage with nothing in it. Both men sat down at the table. "What is this concerning, may I ask?" Ellman asked.

"An employee of yours. John Bryant. He's currently..." Muldoon's answer was cut short when he caught sight of a woman on the lawn with a small dog bouncing along to the tune of its own incessant yapping beside her. She was petite, with pale skin and waves of strawberry blonde hair gathered neatly at the nape of her neck. As far as he was concerned, he was looking at Maggie in a lady's clothing. He quickly looked away and back at Ellman. "He's currently on his way back from South Africa. I wondered if you could tell me what the nature of his trip was and when exactly he will be back?"

"Bryant?" He tilted his head, thinking. "Percy street?"

"Yes, that's the gentleman in question."

"He's overseeing a mining project over there on my behalf. I am not very well, you see." He coughed into a handkerchief, as though on cue. Muldoon leaned back in the chair, trying not to look at Maggie's doppelganger outside. "There was a bit of tension with one of our partners, and Mr Bryant went down to sort it all out. He is due back..." he waved a hand. "I'll have to ask Gladys. Gladys!" he called.

The maid Muldoon had seen before returned to the sunroom and waited for instruction. "Gladys, my dear, please could you fetch me my diary?"

"Yes, sir."

"It's the old gout," Ellman said, indicating at his slippers with his cane. "I can't walk far these days." Ellman was noticeably fat, with a nest of grey hair that circled around a shiny, bald centre. His beard was long, with a curled moustache under his Roman nose. Despite his apparent poor health, the man seemed comfortable, and his cheeks flushed with vigour.

"I came by your offices first thing this morning, sir. Your secretary kindly gave me your address. I need a character statement for Bryant, as he's been away for some time, and I'm not able to ask his wife."

"Oh, why's that?"

"She's quite ill, sir," Muldoon said while the maid gently laid the diary on the table in front of Ellman.

"I'm sorry to hear that." Ellman reached for his spectacles and placed them on the end of his nose. He opened the book and flicked through the pages. "Ah yes, he is due back on Monday next week. November the 28th. He's sailing back on the *Dun-cannon*, it says here."

"Thank you, sir." Muldoon said, writing it down in his note-book. "Now could you tell me about your relationship with Mr Bryant."

"He's my employee. Married. One child. Lives on Percy Street."

"Has he been married before, Mr Ellman?"

"I don't know, Inspector." He eyed Muldoon curiously. "Why would you want to know that?"

"This is a murder investigation, Mr Ellman," Muldoon said, fixing his eyes on Ellman. "John Bryant is our number one suspect."

Ellman's eyes widened in horror. "John Bryant?" he asked, holding his hand to his head. "Bryant?"

"The body of a woman was found this morning at number five, Percy street. I was asked to come here and obtain a character statement from his most recent employer, and that's you."

"Yes, of course." Ellman sat up straight and put his hands together in the wicker chair. "I met him on a return voyage from Australia. Before my health took a turn, I liked to oversee new contracts in person, and I'd set up offices on the gold coast. It was something simple really—a game of cards. We played together a few times and I got to know him. He was affable, with a wife and child back home and I quite liked him. I thought him a promising young man and a keen businessman, so I invited him to buy shares in my company, of which he did, and that was that, really."

Muldoon felt his brows furrowing and made a conscious effort to iron it out. "So you haven't worked with him much?"

"Not really. I asked him to go to South Africa because I couldn't, and he was happy to do it. Probably missed the peace and quiet of life in the goldfields." Ellman laughed, reflecting. "Perhaps family life wasn't for him."

"Perhaps not," Muldoon agreed, looking at the man's dark eyes and wondering where he'd seen them before. Muldoon completed the rest of his statement and bid Ellman farewell. "I'll be in touch if I need anything else."

Ellman sat in the chair, staring into the abyss and said in a quiet voice, "it's such a shame. I quite liked him."

"The case isn't closed yet, sir."

The old man snapped back into consciousness, flushing slightly. "Oh, I thought..."

Muldoon fixed his hat on his head. "Evidence certainly points that way. I'm sure you'll hear about it soon enough."

"What will happen to him, if he is guilty?"

"He'll be hanged of course, Mr Ellman."

"Such a shame." Ellman lowered his head and remained seated. "Why would he throw everything away like that? I'm shocked. Shocked I tell you."

"Good day then, sir." Muldoon tipped his hat and left the sunroom. On his way out, he turned one more time to try and look out into the garden. The girl he'd seen with the dog was gone.

On the train ride back to the city centre, he pulled out his notebook and flicked through it again. The visit to Ellman hadn't been a complete waste of time, but he felt he had walked away from a three course meal still left in want of something more substantial.

Back within the enveloping smog and the ebb and flow of the busy city streets, Muldoon stopped at the bridewell and asked to borrow Constable Lacey. The two of them walked up to the east of the city together. For some time, they didn't exchange a word. Muldoon saw the young man looking back in the direction of the bridewell as they walked on, and sighed.

"Stand down, Lacey. If I was going to go and get my pals, take you down an alley and shoot you, it would have happened by now."

"I'm sorry for calling you a mick, sir."

Muldoon shook his head. "Forget about it."

"Very well, sir. Why do we need to go back there?"

"The murder weapon, Lacey. We don't have it yet."

"Why did you need *me*, sir?"

Muldoon stopped walking and glared at him. "What is this, Lacey? Are you a constable or not?"

"Sorry, sir, it's just that—"

"Look," Muldoon said, "Gill says you're as green as grass but you've got good legs on you." The lanky young man seemed so young to him: barely a boy. "Do something useful. You've seen your first dead body. You're investigating your first murder. Find something interesting and maybe he'll promote you to actual constable instead of punkawallah. How about that?"

Lacey nodded eagerly, still unsure as to why Muldoon wanted to help him.

"Let's get on then."

24

As instructed, none of the occupants of number five had left the premises that morning. A patrolling constable had been stationed to wait outside the house until the investigation was over. He seemed relieved when he saw Muldoon and Constable Lacey approaching the front gate, but his shoulders sank again as soon as Muldoon made it clear to him that he was still on watch.

Mrs Mckinnon let them in and brought them to the parlour room, where Beatrice Larkin was waiting for them. The curtains were still drawn, and Beatrice looked like she hadn't slept in days. "Inspector," she said, standing up. "I have the addresses that you asked for." She held out an envelope addressed to Muldoon. He took it gratefully and slipped it into his inside pocket.

"Constable Lacey," he said quietly. "Would you mind giving us a moment?"

The constable nodded and slid out of the room.

"Thank you, Mrs Larkin," he said, moving over to the window and gently opening the curtains. "I have some other questions, if you don't mind."

Beatrice eyed him in puzzlement and sat back down on the sofa. He looked down at a small porcelain figurine on the window ledge, and moved it away from its precarious position at the edge of the sill.

"Mrs Larkin, do you have the razor?" he asked, looking over to her.

She looked up at him in alarm, feeling her palms sweat. "I did... but I don't any more."

He approached the mantelpiece, gazed into the face of the small clock and compared the time with the time on his pocket watch. The clock hadn't been wound for the week yet. He frowned, realising that Maggie was sloppy as well as sly. "Do you know where it is?"

"No. I put it in the chest at the foot of my bed in case you'd need to see it. When Chief Inspector Gill asked me to hand it over this morning, it was gone."

"Do you know who might have taken it?"

"No. Who would do that?" she asked, horrified. "How bizarre!"

"Lacey," Muldoon called through the open doorway. The young constable walked in and stood to attention, waiting for his next order. "Search the house. Start downstairs. The door's just beside the staircase."

Lacey promptly left the room and could be heard opening the basement door. "Beatrice, do you think there's anyone else involved in this murder besides your son-in-law?" Muldoon asked.

She shook her head. "I don't think... I don't know..." Her bottom lip began to tremble. Muldoon held his breath as he witnessed her begin to break down into choking, gasping sobs. She reached for her handkerchief and collapsed into her hands. "How will I tell her?" he heard her ask. "It'll break her heart."

Muldoon reached out and laid a hand on her arm. "I will tell her, if you'd like. But she has to come off whatever poison she is in the grip of."

Beatrice stopped wailing and looked at him wild-eyed, taking short, laboured breaths to try and steady herself. "What?"

"Your daughter's not possessed, Mrs Larkin, nor do I believe her to be ill. I believe that she has become addicted to opium through the administrations of that quack, Dr Swinson. Please don't let him back in here until we have spoken to her properly." The bell rang just as he'd finished his last sentence. "Hopefully, that'll be the second opinion," he said, rising from the sofa, leaving Beatrice to reflect on the news. He answered the door to a short young man dressed in black with a doctor's bag and a top hat.

"Good afternoon," he said with the manner of a well-bred gentleman beyond his years. "I'm Dr Ablewhite. The Chief Inspector sent for me."

"You look about twelve," Muldoon remarked. Ablewhite laughed and adjusted his steel-framed spectacles.

"Such is my lot in life."

"The patient is upstairs," Muldoon said. "Follow me."

He led the young doctor up to the first floor where Frances was lying in her bed. On the chaise longue, Mrs Mckinnon was knitting some socks. She quickly put them away when the two gentlemen entered, and left the room quietly. "She's addicted to opium. I don't know how to get her off it without killing her," said Muldoon, watching the doctor place his bag down on the chaise longue. Frances looked no different to the opium addicts he had seen rolling around in the slum gutters: she was thin, shivering and dead to the world.

Ablewhite removed his outer clothes and washed his hands at the basin with the pitcher on the sideboard. He approached the bed with his sleeves rolled up and leaned in. "Hello, Mrs Bryant," he said quietly. "I'm Dr Ablewhite. I'm here to help you." He put two fingers on her neck, feeling for her pulse. "Sorry, Mrs Bryant, my hands are rather cold." He gently parted her eyelids with his delicate white fingers and looked at her pupils. "Constricted," he said to himself, and inspected her face closely.

She didn't stir from her stupor. Muldoon put his hands in his pockets. "I don't know how much she takes, doctor, but it's been a few weeks of this, according to her mother."

"Could I see the pills?" he asked. Muldoon opened the drawer of the side table. Inside were several brown bottles of tablets rolling around. Muldoon grabbed them and handed them over the bed to the doctor, who studied the labels intently. "Laudanum, opium... they shouldn't be available in this dose." Young Ablewhite looked up at Muldoon, and swallowed. "Someone's poisoning her."

Every hair on Muldoon's body stiffened. "Can we help her?"

Ablewhite cast a doubtful look on his patient's sallow face. "I can reduce her dose of opium and hope that she can be weaned off. I can't simply take it all away. Patients often experience symptoms far worse than those you get from taking these pills regularly." He untied the restraints from Frances' bruised wrists and gently lowered her hands back down by her side. "I bet that feels better," he said, smiling. The doctor's impressive bedside manner threw into stark relief how uncaring and unprofessional Swinson had been. Angered, Muldoon marched over to the bedroom window, threw the sash up and shouted down to the policeman outside. "Constable. I want Dr Swinson of number seven Percy Street arrested, now! If he's not at home, he has a surgery on Duke Street. Find him."

"Righto," the constable said with a nod. He flew out of the front garden in pursuit, truncheon in hand.

Muldoon returned to the doctor at the bedside. "Doctor, how soon can we have her talking?"

He looked to Frances and then back at the inspector. "Two days, at the earliest? She's going to be very ill, Inspector."

"Stay with her. Charge whatever you have to. Get a nurse to help you, if you need one. Spare no expense on this woman! I'll be back later."

As he approached the final step of the staircase, Lacey emerged from the basement with a bundle of cloth in his hands.

"Sir," he said, offering up the discovery. Muldoon unfolded the cloth to find a razor in Lacey's hands.

"Where?" he asked.

"Under the bed," Lacey said. "The room on the left."

Muldoon's heart felt heavy. "I see," was all he could say. "Excellent. Get it down to the station along with the housekeeper. I'll be right with you."

Lacey wrapped it back up and having asked Mrs Mckinnon to get her shawl, left the house with the old woman. "I didn't put that there, Inspector," she said sternly. Her kind eyes penetrated, telling him he was wrong, and like the eyes of a displeased mother, implied that he ought to know better.

"We'll discuss it at the bridewell, Mrs Mckinnon," he said, reserving emotion.

Lacey held her arm and escorted her out of the hallway. "There's no need for that, young man," she said curtly, shrugging him off. "I'm hardly going to outrun you!"

He promptly let go and they walked together civilly until they were out of sight.

Muldoon returned to the parlour room. Beatrice hadn't left the sofa. "It's all my fault," she said, blubbing.

"Mrs Larkin, Frances is very ill, but she needs you by her side. The doctor upstairs is going to help her. She needs to be weaned off." He knelt down to meet her eye level. "Is there anywhere that you could go with your family for a holiday and some fresh air, to aid her recovery?"

"Where?"

"Somewhere not too far away, in case we have any questions, but not the city. This house is the scene of a murder investigation now. It would be best if none of you were here."

"I understand. We can't go home... what would people think?" She looked at him searchingly, and held her hand to her mouth. Muldoon watched her think of something. She raised her finger. "I can write to my sister in New Brighton? Perhaps we could stay with her. It's just across the river. Is that...?"

"New Brighton is perfect."

"Understandably," she said with a sniff, "Sarah and Elsie cannot go back up there, or be expected to sleep in the nursery any longer. I'll give them my room and I'll..." She started to cry again. "I'll go in with Frances."

Muldoon, finding himself trapped with a wailing woman again, stood at the mantelpiece awkwardly, until Beatrice lifted her head. "Inspector?" she asked, dabbing her eyes again. "What happens now?"

"Well, Frances will get better, hopefully, and we can collect a—"

"No," Beatrice interrupted. "I don't mean that. I mean the girl in the trunk. What happens to her now?"

Muldoon thought of the discoloured, decayed body in the trunk, staring at him with hollow eye sockets and a contorted mouth. "We have to try and find out who she was and what her connection was with John Bryant, Mrs Larkin. Hopefully there are some loved ones out there who are looking for her, but as soon as his ship lands, we'll be speaking to him."

He left the room and waited for a moment in the hallway. There was one more face he needed to see before returning to the bridewell.

Sarah was reading a story to Elsie on the sofa of the drawing room in front of a crackling fire when Muldoon entered, closing the door gently behind him. He quietly sat down on one of the chairs at the back of the room. Elsie looked up for a second and cast her eyes back down at the book. He caught the last of the story.

"And for her selfless act, the little mermaid did not return to the sea as foam. She instead became a spirit, spending three hundred years doing good deeds for others, until she could earn her place in His Eternal Kingdom, forever."

Elsie scrunched her face up. "That's not a happy ending."

"Not all endings are happy, my love," Sarah said, kissing her on the head. Sarah hadn't seen the body, but she had seen the constables carry the trunk down the stairs and, realising that the body of a murdered woman had been above her head as she slept, threw up in the nearest basin. "Sometimes, the endings teach us a lesson. What do you think the lesson was in this one?"

"That she shouldn't have run away from home."

"Why do you think that?"

"She had a daddy and sisters. The witch was bad and she wasn't very happy when she got legs because she couldn't talk.

The prince didn't want to marry her. She shouldn't have run away."

"But she has God's love, in the end. Is that not worth all of the suffering?"

Elsie shrugged, losing interest. "Can we go out today?"

"I'm afraid we can't, darling. The policemen have to do a lot of work today in the house."

"Why?"

Sarah looked nervously over to Muldoon, who cleared his throat. "There were rats in the attic, Elsie. They were eating through all of the house."

The child shook her head slowly in shock. "Not my dolls?"

Muldoon laughed despite himself and shook his head. "No, they didn't eat your dolls."

"Can I see them?"

Muldoon and Sarah looked at one another. "We can't go up there at the moment, Elsie," Sarah said. "But perhaps later..."

"I could go and fetch some, if you'd like?" Muldoon offered. Elsie's little face brightened, illuminated by hope. Knowing that saying 'yes' to a child was always heard as *I'll do it right now*, Sarah gave him an encouraging nod. He left the room.

She quickly followed him out, caught him on the other side of the door and whispered. "There is something you should know."

"What's that then?"

Sarah's eyes shifted around the hallway uneasily. "Someone has been in my dresser, Inspector."

"How do you mean?" he asked, baffled. "I had to look for anything that would be useful for the investigation," he remembered the drawing and shook his head, "but I didn't take anything from the dresser."

She cast her eyes down, demonstrating long brown eyelashes. "Someone has been stealing my underwear."

Muldoon's skin turned from his usual peachy colour to a deep red. "Oh."

"And I wondered if it was—well I don't know—but, this morning, when you told me to dress... I looked everywhere and..." The pink of her cheeks deepened. "I couldn't find my underwear."

He suppressed his emerging thoughts, desperately trying to remain professional. "The maid, perhaps?" he offered.

"No." She shook her head, embarrassed. "I've checked."

He puffed his cheeks out and blew the air from his mouth. "This doesn't really have anything to do with the murder, Miss Jones."

Her face reddened. "No, you're right. I shouldn't have said anything."

He smiled apologetically. "I can't go around asking which constable has been pilfering through your knicker drawer, Miss Jones."

"No, you're quite right. Let's forget about it then. Please." She was gone in a flash, back into the drawing room. The door closed firmly within an inch of his face.

25

It was early evening by the time Muldoon had returned to the bridewell. He was surprised to see Gill waiting for him in the main entrance. "What time do you call this then? I'm waiting to interview Mrs Mckinnon, you know."

"Why do I have to do all these interviews, Gov? What the hell do you need me for?"

Gill straightened. "Well, because you're on the team?"

"You just wanted me to sort the ghost out, didn't you?"

"Well, no..." He raised his hands.

Inspector Muldoon was exhausted. "We found the body." Visibly irritated, he shook his empty cigarette tin. "I'm going out for more cigarettes."

"Please." Gill placed a hand on the wall to bar his exit. "I've no one else." Gill was very tall, but Muldoon could meet his eye level. "There are a lot of questions to ask and—"

"There are at least twenty other bobbies in here, not to mention you've already got detectives—"

"All right!" Gill snapped. "You're my best detective."

Muldoon stared ahead for a moment, hollowed his cheeks in annoyance. "This isn't my chessboard, sir. I don't even work here."

"It's not, but would it be if I told you the head of police wants to throw wages at you that are similar to mine?" He eyed Muldoon for a moment, trying to see what was going on in the mysterious dark head of the Irishman. "He needs more detectives. *Good* detectives. You wouldn't need to dance round any more bags of gold under rainbows, my friend, and none of the twats downstairs are up to it yet. They'd rather watch the horse racing or raid boats and call it a day's work. Not you though. You sneak up on them, disappearing and reappearing like a fucking highwayman. I couldn't ask any of them to sort out a poltergeist or a wolf-bite, could I? Imagine that in the logbook."

Muldoon scoffed. "You're not funny, Gill." His thoughts flashed to his basement office and his cold, dark lodgings under the brothel. "I'm just a consultant. I was happy to help you and all... but... I don't know."

"He wants you Mulders. Special crimes. Think about it."

Muldoon relented. "All right. I promise to think about it, and no more."

Gill's face softened. "Statements then? I've got the house-keeper in there," he said, pointing to his office. "Come on, help me out."

Agreeing that a seven-by-seven foot cell didn't feel like an appropriate place to interview such a sweet old lady as Violet

Mckinnon the housekeeper, Gill had kindly offered up his office and made her a cup of tea. She took it gratefully, and remained impressively calm considering the harsh environment. Next to the high, severe walls, Violet Mckinnon looked tiny and out of place. She dropped a cube of sugar in her cup and gave it a stir, finally ending the ritual with a tiny tinkle of the spoon on the rim of the cup.

"Did you put the razor under your bed, Mrs Mckinnon?" Muldoon asked calmly. Gill scribbled the notes down in the logbook.

"With God as my witness, I did not. Mrs Larkin put it in her room, and that was where it stayed. I laid eyes on it once, and that was when Mrs Larkin had confiscated it. I had never seen it before then. I was informed that Mrs Bryant had found the razor from somewhere and hidden it underneath her pillow." She sipped some tea demurely and continued with, "we worried that Mrs Bryant intended to hurt herself, as can be the way when one is so very ill." She stared down her glasses at the two men.

"Who do you think might have moved it then, Mrs Mckinnon?" Muldoon asked.

"I've no idea."

"Very well." Muldoon leaned back with his arms folded. "Who do you think is responsible for the body in the attic?"

Mrs Mckinnon looked across the desk in genuine surprise, with a hint of a frown above her eyes. "I haven't a clue, Inspector. I've only been with the family since August of this year."

"Is there anybody who could verify that?" Muldoon asked.

"Mrs Bryant, of course," she said, putting her hand to her mouth in thought. "And of course... the directory where the vacancy at Percy Street was advertised." She looked at them, triumphant, with a smile they'd both seen before: the winner of a poker game.

Checkmate, Muldoon thought, smirking. "Did Mr Bryant hire you?"

"No," she said, shaking her head vehemently. "I was hired by Mr Ellman in May. He owned the house at the time."

"Mr Thomas Ellman?"

"Yes, Inspector."

"Ellman as in, Ellman and company?"

"I believe so, Inspector," she said politely.

Muldoon and Gill looked at each other. "Thank you for your time, Mrs Mckinnon," Gill said with the kind of charming smile he'd reserve for his mother. "Please finish your cup of tea while we talk outside for a moment." He closed the door and turned to Muldoon.

"That's interesting," he said.

"What do we do with her then?"

"Let her go."

"Hang on—she says Ellman owned the house. We've got deeds downstairs that say Bryant has owned it since 1882."

Gill stewed on the information for a moment, pursing his lips in thought. "Someone's lying," he grumbled.

Muldoon, thinking of his next move, asked, "has Swinson been brought in yet?"

Gill shook his head. "Phillips has been looking for him. His wife says he's been missing since yesterday. His secretary says the same. Slippery bastard is on the run, I bet. If he doesn't come home by tomorrow, I'm sending a flying squad to find him."

Muldoon grunted with approval.

"I'd be on the run too if I'd been poisoning a woman to death in front of her family," Gill said. "He must know something we don't." He folded his arms. "It's one thing we know Bryant didn't do... but... would he have a doctor do that while he was out of the country?"

"No idea. Maybe he had his eye on another woman."

Gill nodded in agreement. "Toffs again. Divorce is a scandal, but no one bats an eyelid when a spouse dies of 'consumption' weeks before another wife comes along, even if the second one is richer."

As both men turned to walk down the corridor, they heard the swing and slam of a door in the distance and looked up. It was Lacey. "Sir," he said, removing his helmet. "Bryant's ship has been spotted in the bay of Biscay."

Gill rubbed his palms together. "Slowly, slowly, catchy monkey. Let's pray he was even on it." He narrowed his eyes at Muldoon. "If only someone had let me send out a fucking warrant for his arrest."

"And what?" Muldoon snapped. "Have every paper out there slap his face on the front page and let him know that he's a wanted man?"

"It's my investigation!"

"Then what do you need me for?" Muldoon said through gritted teeth.

Lacey looked on uncomfortably as the air in the corridor grew thicker with tension, as it always did when Gill and Muldoon locked horns. Gill glowered at Muldoon, and snapping out of it, jovially pinched his cheek. "Because I've a temper, Mulders. This is why I need you here... Lacey, please take Mrs Mckinnon home and tomorrow, go back and bring that maid in. I want to know what she knows, but tonight, I think I need to get some sleep."

Muldoon licked his lips, thinking of what he was going to say to Mr John Bryant. Gill, with an expression of thunder across his brow, seemed ready to charge in and provide the noose himself. "We don't know if he did it, remember," Muldoon said, unable to tell if he was about to witness a police interview or a bare-knuckle boxing match.

"What?" Gill growled. "We've got the murder weapon, we've got the body, we've got the bastard. What do you mean *we don't know if he did it*?"

"He'll be able to seek counsel, Gov. It's not just some beggar or drunk you pulled in off the street, remember. This man can afford counsel."

Gill rubbed his temples. If he had mutton chops, Muldoon was certain that he would have torn them off by now. "You're right," he sighed. "A profound lack of sleep is clouding my judgement, Mulders. You must forgive me."

"There is nothing to forgive, Gov. I am much the same."

Muldoon hadn't slept for days. Unfortunately for Gill, the bridewell seemed to have experienced an unnatural surge of activity, courtesy of the city's drunkards, smugglers, scrappers, thieves and beggars, all in time for the final week of John Bryant's absence. Gill had hardly been home.

In Muldoon's case, he had been forced awake every night by a recurring visitor: the ghost of Mary. When she was not standing in the corner of his room, she would hover over him as he lay in bed, gripping his throat in her hands and screaming until he woke, gasping for air. Paulie, still lodging with Muldoon, had seemed unaffected by the paranormal activity, much to Muldoon's chagrin. At times, he even found himself resenting the drunkards sleeping the night away in the cells. What she wanted, he couldn't tell, and he learned to live with her presence hovering over him, watching every step he took.

Gill slid the hatch to the left to make sure they had the right one. He made an approving guttural sound and turned to Muldoon. "Handsome bastard, isn't he?"

"Wait, Gov," Muldoon said, feeling the rush of adrenaline in his core. He pulled out his notebook and presented Gill with Sarah Jones' drawing. Muldoon looked from drawing to detainee and frowned. "It... it can't be," Muldoon said under his breath. The man in the drawing was almost identical, save for a few minor differences across the nose and hairline. Bryant did not have a moustache like the subject of the sketch.

The two inspectors entered the cell, causing an already nervous John Bryant to back further into the corner. "Evening, Bryant," Gill said.

John Bryant looked up at them with wild, frightened eyes. "What's this all about? Where is my family?"

Muldoon took his chance to get a look at his eyes. They were grey. Noticeably grey, and the same eyes he'd seen on Elsie Bryant.

"You're in here for the murder of a woman at number five, Percy street," Gill said.

Muldoon watched the man's face turn ghostly pale despite a fresh band of sunburn across his nose. "No," was all John Bryant could say. "No, it can't be."

Muldoon sensed the chief relish in the discomfort he was thrusting upon the detainee, and gave him a discouraging glare. Gill registered it and said, "No, not Frances Bryant."

"Thank God," Bryant said, dropping his head into his hands.

"Have you not heard from your wife recently, Mr Bryant?" Gill asked, leaning against the wall.

Bryant shook his head. "No. I feared the worst."

Gill pondered for a moment, and lit his pipe. "Why would you fear the worst, Mr Bryant? Everything all right at home?"

John Bryant, his mouth agape, shook his head again.

"You mean everything isn't all right at home?" Gill prodded. "Which is it, Bryant?" He pulled his pipe from his mouth and growled, "Bryant! Answer me."

"I... I didn't know the address of where I was going. Ellman said he'd write to my wife with the address. Then, when I didn't receive anything, I decided to write to her and... I didn't get a response." He ran his fingers through his uncombed hair. "I knew it would take a while for anything to get to me and the journey back was so long that... I thought perhaps she felt she'd just wait it out. She wasn't particularly pleased when I informed her of the trip and, well you know how women can hold their grudges. I'd hoped it was just Frances giving me the silent treatment. I only started to worry when there were police waiting for me on the jetty."

"Is there..." Muldoon thought back to the man Frances described in her letters. "Is there any chance, Mr Bryant, that your wife's affections could have gone elsewhere?"

"What?" Bryant asked, frowning. "Why would you... why would you say that?"

Muldoon, distracted, looked around the cell. Unlike absolutely everywhere else he had travelled that week, the ghost of Mary hadn't appeared. She met him at coffee houses, in taverns, on the street when he was about to cross, or in his nightmares. She was nowhere to be seen on this occasion, and he wondered why. He had grown used to the harassment, and her absence made him anxious.

"Everything all right there, Inspector?" Gill asked, wondering what the hell he was doing. "Is the brickwork to your standards?"

"Sorry, Gov," Muldoon said, checking behind him. John Bryant remained seated; he was looking at them expectantly, waiting for someone to talk.

Gill spoke first. "John Arthur Bryant. Do you know who is responsible for the dead woman who's been in your attic for years?"

"No," Bryant said, dumbfounded.

Gill sucked the air through his teeth as though Bryant's answer caused him physical pain. "Mr Bryant, it is incredibly likely that you will be hanged for the murder of this woman whether you tell us her name or not, so if you have even a modicum of decency, you'll tell us what we want to know: who is she and what was she doing stuffed in a trunk in your attic?"

"I don't know what you're talking about," he said, looking between each of them. "I've only owned that house since May of this year... But I should like to speak with a solicitor before I continue."

"Fine," Gill said, turning to the door. "As is your right."

Muldoon hung back for a moment and crouched down to Bryant's level. "In her letters that she wrote to you, Mr Bryant... she described being able to see you through the keyhole? If it wasn't you... I just thought..." Bryant looked down at the floor, devastated. "But your wife is seriously ill, Bryant," Muldoon added. "And it could well have been a fever dream."

Bryant lifted his face up to meet Muldoon's. "Can I see her?"

Muldoon regretfully shook his head. "Not yet."

Bryant, realising that Frances may not have even wanted to see him considering the circumstances, nodded in reluctant acceptance. "Please may I see these letters?" he asked.

"Of course, Mr Bryant. I'll have them brought to you, but they're evidence, so you must read them under supervision and hand them back."

Bryant nodded. "Thank you," he said quietly. Muldoon rose and left the cell where Gill was waiting to close the door with a ceremonious, thunderous bang. A warden approached with the ring of keys and locked it.

"He's confused about the body, Gov," Muldoon said quietly. "He hasn't a clue what we're talking about."

Gill stared at him in disbelief. "Piss off. He's doing the confused husband act, that's all. Don't fall for it."

Muldoon returned to Percy street where, just a couple of days before, he had said a silent farewell to the Bryant household. Concealing himself in the shadows of the shedding trees he stood beneath in the churchyard, he observed their departure from afar. Beatrice, Frances, Sarah and Elsie piled into a cab without issue; he watched the wheels roll along Percy Street as the cab headed down the hill on the road that would lead them to the ferry terminal. Silently, he wished them well. When he turned to look at number five again, he saw Mary standing on the front path. From the other side of the road, he couldn't see her eyes clearly, but he felt the weight of them. She was angry. With him, or with something else, he didn't know. "Enough," he said under his breath, and walked instead to number seven.

A maid brought him into Mrs Swinson's parlour room where she was sitting with her half-finished embroidery piece: some silk bouquet arrangement. "Inspector, thank goodness. Have you found my husband?" she asked, placing it down into a basket beside her chair.

Muldoon felt his stomach sink and realised he hadn't thought of how Mrs Swinson would feel. His focus had always been on the doctor. "I am sorry, Mrs Swinson," he said earnestly with his hat in his hands. "We have been unable to find your husband."

Wonderful, another blubbering woman, he thought as he watched her crumple into a sobbing mess, covering her doughy face in her hands.

"I do need to ask you a few questions about his habits and relationships, if that's possible."

The older, silver-haired lady blew her nose hard into a handkerchief, making him flinch. Calmly, he presented Swinson's small diary from his inside pocket and placed it on the coffee table. She looked up at him and then down at the diary. "What is that?"

"It's your husband's diary," he said.

"Where did you get that?"

"He'd left it at his office," he lied.

Mrs Swinson shook her head in disbelief. "It wasn't there when I looked. Where did you find it?"

"I didn't, Mrs Swinson. One of my constables did. It must have slipped down the side of something, or been too well-hidden in a drawer." She seemed unconvinced, but composed herself anyway. "I would like to know," Muldoon began, "if there is anything in this that would suggest where he may have disappeared to."

Mrs Swinson picked it up and flicked through the pages. "Try looking at the last seven days," Muldoon suggested, "and tell me if there's anything interesting here." He watched the lines in her forehead deepen as she mouthed words and letters she read. She scanned the pages and seemed puzzled. "This isn't his diary."

"Is it not?"

"I mean," she nodded, "it is his handwriting, but it's not the one he uses for appointments. I don't know what this one is for."

"Do any of the initials mean anything to you?"

She shook her head again. "No. I'm sorry, Inspector. It might as well be written in Swahili. I'm sorry."

Muldoon's eyes widened as he caught sight of something on the page as it rested in her hands. "May I?" he asked. She gave it back to him and he turned the book upside down.

Muldoon looked closer. It was an address. *Christ, how did I miss that?*

Muldoon stepped off the train at Gateacre station and, unsure of where exactly to go, made his way up the hill and stopped at The Black Bull public house immediately. It rested in the centre of the hilltop village like a beacon, glowing white in the autumn sunshine with its mock-Tudor stucco and black beams.

Sitting in a warm corner of the pub beside its blazing hearth, he opened his notebook and reviewed his notes. He copied the upside-down address into his own notebook and tore the sheet of paper out. When the young barmaid brought him his lunch, he asked her if she knew where he could find the house on the piece of paper. She informed him that the house of interest was almost opposite, in one of the cottages further up the hill. He thought of his next move over some mashed potatoes and a pint of brown ale.

The village of Gateacre was lively, with cart horses dominating the main road. A herd of sheep passed down the hill as he dined, accompanied by a farmer and a slinking, swift collie that reminded him of Paulie McCrae. The farmer raised his cap to the pub landlord who was opening the hatch for the new load of barrels, courtesy of the brewery opposite. As well as its rustic charm, the village was as lush as Allerton had been. Crisp, decaying leaves sailed down to the ground like confetti on the shining cobbles.

A stomach full of hot food and a drink had made Muldoon feel drowsy. He braced himself for returning to the bright yet cold autumn air outside.

With a deep breath, Muldoon crossed the road passing a couple of shops, a chapel and another inn. Finding the sandstone cottage he was looking for, he knocked on the door and stood back. To his surprise, the door was not opened by a maid, but by Dr Swinson himself.

The two men stared at each other for a moment. Swinson, fully dressed in his black suit, blinked a few times before greeting Muldoon.

"Night duty with a patient, doctor?" Muldoon asked.

Before Swinson could speak, they both heard a child calling from the hallway. "Who is it, Daddy?"

Having kindly been afforded the guise of going to a business meeting for the sake of his secret family, Swinson accompanied Muldoon back to The Black Bull, where they sat down in a quiet corner, shadowed by unlit lamps. The barmaid, recognising Muldoon again, flashed him a coquettish smile from behind the bar as she dried a glass. He approached and ordered coffee to be brought to his table. She appeared within minutes, taking longer than was necessary to place the coffee on the table, and reappeared a minute later asking if they needed any sugar. Muldoon declined, leaving it to Swinson to deal with her. He didn't want sugar either. Having no reason to stay, she disappeared from view back to her work.

Swinson sat across from him, representing a shadow of the man he had seen at Percy Street. He spoke quietly, fixing his fearful eye on the Inspector. His body slumped against the back of the huge chair, making the large man seem pathetically small. "He would have told my wife if I didn't do as he said," Swinson said, holding his coffee cup with a trembling, fat hand.

"You were poisoning Mrs Bryant, Swinson."

Swinson fought against the urge to give way to his emotions and pushed his lips together for a moment. When he had taken a breath, he said, "I didn't intend for this to happen. What must you think of me?"

Muldoon raised an eyebrow, wondering what that had to do with the crime he was concerned with, but allowed him to continue nonetheless. "You can't help who you fall in love with, and I couldn't bring myself to divorce Sally... You know, we lost eight children? All eight of them." Swinson's bottom lip finally overpowered him as he spoke with a waver in his voice. "It destroyed her. I couldn't divorce her. She had nothing."

"So what, you shacked up with your secretary?"

"I was grieving," he snapped like a wounded animal, then immediately softened, looking into the distance with a mournful voice. "Our youngest, Paul. He was the only one to live beyond infancy and... he was at University in Liverpool. We followed him over here eventually, a few years ago. Then consumption took him soon after. I didn't mean to do what I did, but I worked long hours and when Elizabeth told me she was with child—*my child*, I wanted to be with her. It felt like a miracle, with her being forty and surviving the pregnancy. I couldn't just... I couldn't just ignore that. I have a son. God gave me a son."

Muldoon sipped his coffee pensively.

"And Ellman knew about your second family, then?"

Swinson nodded. "He said he would tell the papers if I didn't help him. I'd lose everything."

"Why did he want you to hurt Mrs Bryant?"

Swinson looked at him desperately. "I don't know."

"Who called you to come to the house?"

"The maid."

"Maggie?"

"I don't know her name. The little, peaky-looking one in the lace cap. She said she had instructions from her employer. Look—please—he'll destroy me. That'll be my wife, my mistress and my son on the street."

Muldoon, finding sympathy he didn't know was there, asked, "can you prove that you were blackmailed, doctor?"

Swinson nodded gravely. "I kept the letters, but I didn't know what I could do with them. The man's power seems to have no limit, but I kept them, just in case."

Muldoon stood, and said, "write to your wife, doctor." He spoke quietly, not wanting his words to land on the other ears in the room. "She's worried sick. Don't put an address on the letter, because there are eyes everywhere looking for you." He leant down and spoke in the doctor's ear. "You're wanted for attempted murder."

The doctor gawped at the inspector, who stood up straight again, adjusted his suit and followed up with, "I may be able to sort this out, but I need your cooperation. Bring the letters to the Main Bridewell by tomorrow morning, or you'll be tried for the attempted murder of Frances Bryant. Hurry, doctor. We don't have much time."

"Understood," the doctor whispered. "Thank you, Inspector—wait, Mrs Bryant—Will she be all right?"

"She's with another doctor now. Whether she recovers or not is in God's hands, no thanks to you." Muldoon secured his hat on his head and said, "but if she dies, doctor... the charge is murder."

He left the doctor alone to drink his lukewarm coffee in silence.

26

Dear John,

Yesterday, I awoke as though from an enduring, terrible dream. Mother has brought us to New Brighton, under doctor's orders. As I'd tried to tell her all along, Swinson was poisoning me, and every day I was sick or feverish. I loathe that man. I knew he'd try to kill me in the end, whether it be through dull conversation or other means. She is beside herself with grief. I forgive her. She wasn't to know.

Ablewhite has been so kind and attentive. He says I shall make a full recovery, but it will take some time. I am thin, and I do not like to look upon myself in the mirror, for I look... I look like *her.*

Mother wouldn't tell me when I asked where you were. I hoped that it was the 28th of November. No one would confirm what date it was, which I thought was odd, and I could not find a single letter or newspaper in the house.

As I was not at home, I asked when I could see you, but nobody seemed to have an answer with which they could provide me. I feared the worst: your death.

It was cool outside with a brisk wind, but overall, not terribly cold. We went for a walk along the pier. Elsie skipped ahead and flew her kite on the sands! She is ever so good. She misses you. I have embraced that child more times in this past week than I have in all of her life, because she is all I have right now to keep me alive.

I've never been on this side of the river before—I could almost see our house from the golden beaches! Hundreds of vessels entered and exited the river, tooting and puffing with their characterful sounds. I wondered which one you were on, and I wept, because I cannot bear to be apart from you.

On the way back to my aunt's house—against mother's wishes—I happened to find a paper boy, and I looked down at the paper he gave me, and it gave me quite a start. I had not expected to see my husband's face on the front page. Mother rushed to hold me as I fell to my knees. *It cannot be!* I cried. *It cannot be!*

They say you are to be hanged for the murder of a woman found in *our home*. I cannot believe it. I will not believe it. The only fact in this matter is that I have to write to you as you wait in your cell. The doctor does not advise me to cross the river to come to you. I sense no deception—he is good mannered and I am frail.

With what strength I have left in this weak body,
I will fight for you. Mother, and every reputable
name she knows is behind you, John. I have a
new found passion in my soul that is indefatiga-
ble, and they will not take you from me. I have
written to our solicitor. Hold fast, John.

All my love,

Frances

Fred Wilcox arrived at the bridewell the following day. His
arrival prompted a heated discussion between Muldoon and
Gill, as both had forgotten to let him know that they didn't
need a statement any more. "I don't know, sir," Muldoon said
uneasily. "I mean, why do we need a statement from the night
they messed around with a ouija board?"

"A statement's a statement. Don't we need proof that she was
poisoned? He might know something."

Muldoon rolled his eyes. "It just doesn't seem relevant now that the body's been found. The haunting is over." He didn't believe his own words as he heard them, and he hadn't checked since they removed Mary's body from the property. The sudden disappearance of the ghost worried him. If he'd caught the killer, he felt she had no need to bother him. If he hadn't, he worried she'd come back with a vengeance. He buried the thought.

"We can't tell him that. He's come all the way here. Anyway, I've not slept for two days in case you haven't noticed, and my men are still out looking for The Grim Reaper. I'm nipping home for a kip."

"About that, sir," Muldoon said, feeling his heart rising into his throat. Gill looked at him expectantly. "I found the doctor. Tell the squad to stand down."

"Well where is he, then?"

"I just need him for a bit longer, and then he's all yours," Muldoon lied. "Let's get Bryant put away first."

Gill, too tired to think about it, nodded and left the corridor. "Good luck, Mulders. You know where to find me."

Muldoon stepped in to Gill's office where Fred Wilcox was waiting for him, sipping a cup of tea. Muldoon shook off his fatigue, greeted the man and shook his hand before they both sat down.

"Mr Wilcox, thanks for coming in. I believe I need to collect a statement from yourself regarding the night of the seance."

Wilcox tilted his head. "Oh? I thought I was here about John Bryant?"

"John Bryant?"

"Yes. I'm a solicitor. The family has asked me to appoint a barrister who will represent him in court."

Muldoon raised an eyebrow, wondering how Frances was. It had been over a week since he last saw her. "They have?"

"Yes. Put simply: There isn't enough evidence for us to believe it's him."

"Is that so?"

"They will fight the charges."

Muldoon, smelling blood, leaned forward. "We have the murder weapon, Mr Wilcox."

Wilcox remained upright, looking Muldoon directly in the eyes. Fred was bold and assertive, albeit the epitome of friendliness and professionalism as he sat across the desk from the inspector. "I've heard that, yes. But it proves nothing."

"Come again?"

"The brand, Inspector. Where *can't* you find a Sheffield-made straight razor in this country? It could be anyone's."

He was right. He had reason to believe that it was the same brand of razor that John Bryant used, but both his mother-in-law and his housekeeper added that they weren't entirely sure. "He cleaned and sharpened his own razors," Mrs Mckinnon said. Muldoon knew that even if they had confirmed it as the same razor Bryant used: on its own, it proved nothing.

Muldoon made a note of Wilcox's comment, and decided to change the subject.

"Who do you think murdered this woman then? We have Bryant's name on the deeds."

"And I shall be refuting that. There is a copy of his marriage certificate in the post as we speak. Mrs Bryant is adamant that the signature on the deeds is not that of her husband's, and I have more."

"All right, I'm listening."

"Mrs Bryant, as you know, was gravely ill," Fred began. *Was*— that was good news. "And on the night of the seance, we *all* saw that ghost. But the thing is," Fred's eyes twinkled with excitement. "I've seen this woman before."

Wilcox pulled out an envelope and handed it to Muldoon. "It was distributed by the Salvation Army last Christmas in their missing persons campaign. They do it every year, as you may know. Anyway, I was coming out of St Mary's On Christmas Eve and they handed out some photographs as they always do. This is Mary Hobbs—well, I believe the ghost to have been Mary Hobbs. This girl has been missing since November, 1885."

Muldoon gazed at the photo, feeling his hands tremble, and turned it over. The handwriting on the back said *Mary Hobbs, missing since 1885, aged eighteen years.* He turned it over once more; looking up at him was the woman who had been dragged up the stairs. He had no reason to believe that this wasn't the face of the apparition that they called *Mary*. She had been incredibly striking, with masses of dark hair and fine clothes. Around her neck rested a necklace that made his heart thump through his chest. "That necklace," he said, tapping the photograph. "That necklace was on the body we found…" There was more life in the eyes of the still image than there had been any time he'd seen Mary Hobbs. "What else do you know about her?" Muldoon asked, musing.

Fred shook his head heavily. "Not much. Daughter of a wealthy cotton merchant. I've heard of class-defying romances—I mean, I've read *The Greenwood Tree* for goodness' sake and Bryant is married to a schoolmistress, yes—but a sheep-farmer in West Derby and a middle class girl from Allerton? There are more than five miles between them!" He lowered his shoulders. "I've struggled to find any dates that would put them together, or even places where they would cross paths. No mutual friends or connections… I thought of writing to the parents, but to write about what? I couldn't face them as—how could I explain? 'Hello, I've seen your missing daughter and she's rather dead, I'm afraid.' I didn't know what to say. I'm no clairvoyant, and I was hardly going to drag my father-in-law out to Allerton to try and reconnect the family. They would have thought us mad! It was rather a difficult situation. I've only partaken in seances that have been *requested*. We don't doorstop people."

Muldoon, barely listening, stared at the face in his hands. He couldn't take his eyes off the photograph. She had been trying to tell him all along. "Could Frances communicate with her?"

"Absolutely. I'd never seen anything like it. I knew from my father-in-law—Mr Kingsley—that Mrs Larkin had the sight, slightly, but Frances saw her and felt her just as you or I would be aware of each other's presence right now." Fred smiled. "She's rather beautiful isn't she? Don't tell my wife, but if one could fall in love with a photograph, it would be this one."

"Mr Wilcox," Muldoon began, "as part of this investigation, I've been privy to the correspondence between Frances and her husband. In a couple of the letters, Mrs Bryant mentions another ghost. A man? Did the second ghost come up at all in the seance?"

Wilcox shook his head with a downturned mouth. "Not that I am aware of. There was no sign of an additional ghost, Inspector—just this lady, Mary."

Muldoon leaned back in the chair and reflected on the information. "Did Mrs Larkin mention a second ghost?"

Just as Wilcox was about to say "no," there was an urgent knock on the door. Muldoon excused himself and answered to an older constable holding a stack of letters. "Sir," he said. "We was cleaning up in Percy street and Lacey found these in the attic, sir."

"Thanks, Pinners," Muldoon said. "Are you all finished there now?" he asked.

"Yessir, it's all done."

"Thanks," Muldoon took the bundle from him and closed the door. Unable to help himself, he put the letters down on the desk and started reading them. Fred Wilcox twiddled his fingers and looked on awkwardly, wondering if he should excuse himself or not.

The detective bent over them, his dark brows furrowed as he read the words in the letters intently.

"Hang on—" Muldoon said, raising his head for once. "Did you say *Allerton*?"

"Yes." Wilcox nodded. "The Hobbs family resides in Allerton..." Fred's eyes shifted uncomfortably. "Do you need a moment, sir? Is everything all right?"

Muldoon shot up out of his chair and paced the room to the window and back. "You're telling me this woman has been missing since '85, her family are in Allerton and here I am reading letters she wrote to..." he picked up a letter and read it again in a quiet voice. "Margaret Ross...in 1888."

Wilcox waited for the detective to elaborate, but he didn't. Instead, there was another awkward silence followed by Muldoon clearing his throat. "Mr Wilcox, if Bryant's not our man... how would you like to solve a murder with me?"

The next day, Fred was waiting for him in the main reception with a copy of John Bryant's marriage certificate in his hand. Muldoon had a copy of the deeds to five Percy Street in his inside pocket. They both presented the documents to Gill who agreed they didn't seem like the same signatures, at all. Wilcox also had a handful of letters that Frances Bryant had given him upon visiting New Brighton the day before. "Fine," Gill huffed. "I'll send for a handwriting... what are they called again?"

"A graphologist, sir," Wilcox said, smiling.

"Yeah, one of them. I'll get one from the University."

Muldoon and Wilcox left Gill to his work and crossed the street. Hailing a hansom cab to take them to Lord Street, they disembarked and stood before a small office bearing the sign, "Jessops and Partners,"—a sign that was identical to the header of the letter that had been in Muldoon's pocket, signed by Jessops himself.

Inside, a well-groomed male secretary greeted them, had them wait ten minutes while Jessops finished up with another client, and brought them to the office of Michael Jessops. "Thank you, James," said Mr Jessops, watching the younger man leave the room with a longing glance that made Wilcox look again.

Wilcox, doing most of the talking, encouraged Jessops to jog his memory and fetch a copy of the deeds for Percy Street. Jessops, more than happy to help, retrieved a copy from the basement himself and returned to his office. "Yes, John Bryant, 1882 it says here," Jessops said, laying the document down on the desk for Muldoon to read over.

"Thank you for this. It's been ten years Mr Jessops, and I know that you must be rather busy with clients, but I did wonder if you could help us identify him?" Muldoon presented Jessops with his most earnest expression of which Jessops couldn't help but find attractive.

"Well, you're right, Inspector. It has been a while." Fred watched as Muldoon seemed to bat his long black eyelashes at Jessops, rendering him defenceless. "Of course. I'll give it a try," Jessops said, winking.

"I can't thank you enough for your cooperation," Muldoon said, pulling a photograph out of his pocket. He placed the photograph of a dark-haired, handsome man with a moustache on the desk. He was wearing a top hat and dressed as smartly as any banker or company director walking past the offices they sat in. Jessops tilted his head, looking at the photograph intently.

"Yes, that's him," he finally said after some time. "I'd recognise him anywhere." He shot a second glance at the image that Muldoon had placed on the desk. "That's Mr John Bryant."

"Excellent," Muldoon smiled and shook Jessops' hand. "Thank you for your time, Mr Jessops," he said. "Would you be so kind as to just write a note saying we were here? It's just that, with the police service being the way it is..."

"Not at all," said the solicitor. "My secretary—Richard—he can do it."

Wilcox stood and opened the door slightly. "Oh," he said, looking disappointed. "He's with a client. We really have to get back. Do you think you could...?"

Jessops nodded, and said, "yes, of course." He pulled a card from his drawer and scribbled a note with his signature on it, and slid it to Wilcox who had returned to the desk. "It was good to see you again, Fred."

"Likewise," Wilcox said, shaking his hand enthusiastically. "It's been too long."

"A friend of yours?" Muldoon asked him when they had stepped back outside onto the street. Wilcox blushed. "Not quite. He was my principal. He had a few of us under his tutelage and became enamoured with one of my peers."

"They let women train in those days?"

Wilcox smiled uncomfortably. "I didn't say the peer was a woman, Inspector."

"Oh."

"Anyway," Wilcox said, putting his hat on. "What do we do now?"

Muldoon took the calling card out of his pocket and said, "we find out who really signed it."

"It was a risk doing that. He could have seen that photograph in the paper!"

"But he didn't, did he?" Muldoon winked. They both looked down at the photograph they had shown Jessops. Borrowed from a reporter friend at *The Post,* the photograph had been attached to the obituary of a James T. Wallace. Muldoon grinned. "He's never seen John Bryant before in his life, or this deceased son of a coal tycoon, clearly—what have you got there?" he asked, looking at the document Wilcox had produced from the wallet under his arm.

He looked at him mischievously, and asked, "you don't think Jessops writes all his own letters and contracts, do you?" Wilcox grinned. "I pinched this one when his secretary went back into his office."

"Fred, you snake." Muldoon laughed, impressed.

"Well then," the smaller man said, sticking his chest out, "let's go and hand these in."

"Why are you doing this?" Gill asked, slapping his hands on the desk in exasperation. "He's *downstairs*."

"I'm just not convinced, Gov."

"Mulders," Gill barked. "I've got the head of police breathing down my neck wanting this thing put to bed. Bryant's face is all over the papers." Gill slammed the newspaper down on the desk. One of the front page headlines read: 'Shear evil: sheep farmer murders first wife and locks her in the attic.' Muldoon rubbed his forehead for a moment.

"They always exaggerate. We have no proof."

"The deeds, Mulders!" Gill exploded. "We've got the fucking deeds!"

"Forgery and framing."

"What? Can you prove it?"

"Not yet. I handed some more evidence to the graphologist."

"That's not going to work! It's not even a proper job. Hand-writing expert? Isn't that what a school teacher does? It's a fad."

"What about Geography then? His time in Australia? Mrs Bryant has letters he sent when he was in Australia."

Gill pursed his lips in thought, acknowledging his defeat. "Why are you doing this?"

"Because you're happy to have an innocent man hanged, Gov. I can't—"

"This is *how it works*, Mulders. We find the body, we pin the murder on the most likely and we get rid. Keeps the city happy."

"You know it's not right. We can't just go on circumstantial evidence. There's something else going on here."

Gill looked up at the ceiling and let his shoulders collapse. "Who did it then, clever Dick?"

"I don't know yet."

"Then why are you wasting my time?" Gill roared, squaring up to him. Muldoon stood still, challenging him with a stern glare. Gill relented, and sat back down, massaging his temples. "You've got three days, Muldoon. Three days. Head of police wants this dealt with, and I can't keep it open for a hunch."

27

Dear Maggie,

I fear that the day is due when he will not let me out again. I have had to convince him to let me see a doctor, privately. The walk to the surgery is good exercise, and he cannot argue that it isn't beneficial for me. I always come back within two hours, and he is learning to trust me, but I know him, and he will revert to his true nature again. It is in the waiting room of the surgery that I write these letters to you. I stop by a hotel and ask the concierge to post them for me. He is happy to do so, and asks how he can assist me further. The kindness of strangers! It is a balm to my soul.

I cannot come home, because he will find me, and I cannot begin to think what he would do to anyone who tried to protect me from him. I made my bed, and I must lie in it.

There is not much time, but I still wish to proceed with the plan. It breaks my heart, and I wish things could be different. This is not the life that I dreamed of, and it is certainly not the life I would have left my family for. For that I am a fool. I shall regret it for the rest of my life.

I do not deserve your loyalty and love, but I am grateful to God for you and Sissy and all you do for me, and all you will do for me in the years to come.

My eternal love,

Mary

THE HEAVY, OPPRESSIVE ODOUR of factory smoke accompanied by dense clouds from the chimneys blanketed the mid-morning autumn sun as Muldoon approached the east side of the city. Crossing the street, he weaved his way through the shopkeepers, residents and restaurateurs of Chinatown, where he found the tea house he had been asked to wait in. He sat down and informed the waiter that he was hanging on until his company arrived, and positioned himself so that he could see the world pass by from a table near the window. Faces of every age, sex and colour seemed to pass along the glass panes, but he didn't see the one he was hoping to meet.

"We can't talk here," Maggie had said when he caught her turning the corner of Percy street the previous day.

Muldoon took stock of the bruises on her forearm as she pulled away from him. She had tucked it back into her shawl. "Who did that to you?" he asked.

She shook her head, eyes wide with fear. "Nobody. I knocked it."

He wanted to interview her there and then but she wouldn't speak any more. "It's not safe," she said, looking down the street and back at him. "I can't go back with you. Please. I can't."

"All right," Muldoon said, accepting defeat. "But I think you know something about the woman in the box, Maggie." A fire rose in his belly, as he dared to say, "I think you knew Mary."

Maggie fixed her eyes on him, and looked as though she was going to faint. She helplessly clutched the basket she was holding, as though it could steady her. "Not here. Please. It's not safe."

She agreed to meet him the following morning at the tea house. "In Chinatown. No one expects to see me there," she said.

He waited for nearly two hours.

He rang the bell several times and peered in through the window of number five, Percy Street. He couldn't see anything through the closed curtains; he tried the back gate and found all of the back doors and windows impenetrable. Frustrated, he returned to the front of the house and stood on the top step. At any moment, a patrolling constable would pass and he would borrow him for a moment.

The day was clear and dry, and the mid-morning sun warmed his face as he waited on the top step of the porch. In the still, eerie silence of the morning, he fancied he could hear movement inside, and listened against the glass. The thumping of footsteps and breaking of crockery grew louder until he heard a woman scream.

"Maggie?" he asked, banging on the door. "Maggie?"

He stepped back and lunged at the door, trying desperately to kick it in. He ran at it again and again until a constable grabbed him by the shoulders and asked "what do you think you're doing?"

"Oh, I'm..." Muldoon pulled out his badge. "I'm an inspector. Help me get this door down."

The constable helped him break the door down, issuing the final blow to the lock with his truncheon. Muldoon burst into the house past him, looking for the owner of the scream.

He found Maggie lying on the parlour room floor, her neck slashed open. The razor, tossed carelessly on the wood floor, lay only a few inches from her head.

Muldoon was still at the scene of the murder after Maggie's body had been covered and taken away in a wagon. The familiar, metallic smell had started to fade as the blood congealed on the floor.

Having the entire house to himself, he passed through each room, waiting. Only the grandfather clock ticked in the hallway. The body had been discovered just after twelve o'clock, and it was now half past one in the afternoon. "Mary?" he asked quietly. Nothing about the hallway changed. He stood and stared at the great mechanical face for a few minutes more.

He decided to try something. Winding the clock back by ninety five minutes, he waited for the long hand to land. It struck twelve. He touched it.

As clear as it had been the first time, the vision from the days before presented itself again. Against an unknown force, he pushed his way towards the foot of the stairs, leaning as far as he could to try and get closer to the man dragging Mary's body away. The clock struck for the twelfth time and threw him out of the vision. He blinked and found himself back at the park bench with Sarah, moments before she caught him looking at the sketch book. "What are you doing?" she asked. Before he could answer, he was back in her alcove of the nursery looking through her sketchbook. He flicked through page after page furiously as the small shape of a pencil-drawn stick man in the corner ran to the next page, and the next. The man with no face. He was in her dresser, rubbing his forefinger and thumb against the soft muslin fabric of her undergarments. He held a chemise up and sniffed it, but he wasn't holding it with his own hands. He was somebody else. He heard himself breathing heavily, standing over Sarah as she slept. A desire for her burned deep within him, and he couldn't suppress it. He reached for his trousers and started to unfasten them, until a shadow moved in his peripheral vision.

When he turned his head to catch sight of the figure standing on the other side of the bed, he froze. Mary was staring at him: her eyes dark and focused, even hateful. She lifted her hand, pointing to him. Her scream seemed to shatter his ear drums as he fell to the floor with his hands over his head.

Muldoon lay on the nursery floor, feeling his pulse hammering through his body. His head ached, and he couldn't get up for some time. He moved his eyes around the room and saw that he had an audience of dolls and a rocking horse watching him. Rolling over and feeling ashamed at the sight of his unbuttoned trousers, he managed to balance and put his weight into his palms and knees, eventually pushing up onto his feet.

On the floor beside him was the calling card that Sarah had given to him. He checked his pockets and saw that it was the same one. He flipped it over.

Sarah's scent still lingered in his nostrils, and he stared down at his hands. They were his again, and there was nobody in the nursery but him.

Downstairs, he stood for a moment on the top step of the porch before another constable and a joiner with a bag of tools and some timber over his shoulder approached. "We just need to put a lock on it, sir. Don't want no looters."

"Aye, absolutely," he said, looking back at the house. He stepped aside, letting them pass. As the joiner got to work on the door, Muldoon pulled the card out of his pocket again and made the decision to head back to his office.

"Yeah, I've seen him before," Chloe said, eyeing the sketch he had given her.

"Do you remember what colour his eyes were, Chloe?" Muldoon asked.

She didn't need time to think. "Brown. Brown eyes that were so dark, they were almost black... I'd never forget *those* eyes."

Muldoon looked down at Sarah's drawing again, his stomach still feeling uneasy. "Chloe, I know that usually, that sort of comment would be heard as a compliment, but you're saying it with some disgust in your voice there."

Chloe rolled one of her caramel shoulders towards her ear and looked at Mae, who was listening intently with a look of worry on her face. "You didn't say he was weird, Chloe?" she said, taking a drag of her cigarette.

Chloe shrugged and sat on her hands. "He was, but it was a different kind of weird."

"Did he try to hurt you?" Muldoon asked.

She shook her head, loosening wisps of midnight hair across her shoulders. "No, not like that. He likes to... you know... do stuff to the clothes and things."

"Oh?" Mae asked with a raised eyebrow.

"Yeah. Not watching me do it or anything. He comes in, puts some stuff on the bed that he's brought and asks me to leave him. The first time he came here, he looked through my dresses and laid one on the bed. I asked him if he wanted me to put it on. He just said no and told me to get out. He didn't shout at me or anything. That's why I'm saying he didn't seem dangerous. I just mean he was weird as in, not interested in you know...me?"

Madame Chloe was Mae's most expensive whore, and Muldoon could see why. She was different from the other girls, with a slight French twinge to her accent, and the beautiful, round face of a North African angel, embellished with large, almond eyes. The girl was sought after by the wealthiest men in the city, being far too expensive for a sailor's pay grade, or as Lacey had discovered, a police officer's. "What sort of things did he bring with him?" Muldoon asked.

"Someone else's clothes. Chemise and drawers, that kind of thing."

Muldoon felt his stomach drop. "Do you have any of them still?"

Chloe nodded. "I just kept them in case he forgot them and wanted them back. I didn't wear them or nothing."

She stretched a long, elegant arm out and opened a drawer from her dresser. Lifting out some delicate items in a bundle, she passed them to Muldoon, who held them like they had been a newborn child. "All of these?" he asked, surprised at the volume.

"Yeah. He comes here quite often, so I supposed he'd want them back."

Muldoon laid the undergarments on the bed and swallowed. Mae and Chloe watched, intrigued.

He turned everything inside out looking for labels until he found what he didn't want to see. In a pair of lace-trimmed drawers, he found the initials, S.J. He also found her initials in a muslin chemise and lastly, the initials M.H in a silk nightgown.

"I need to take these away, ladies," he said regretfully.

"What if he comes back?" asked Chloe, frowning.

Muldoon thought for a moment. If he came back and found the items where he left them, he would suspect nothing. If he came back and found the items gone, nobody knew how he would react. "I know the owners of these things," he said. "But I doubt they'll want them back, after..." he picked up a chemise that was crumpled; it was unusually stiff—as stiff as a garment that had been starched. Chloe covered her mouth with her hand.

"If he comes here again," Muldoon said, "I need to know."

"Why?" asked Chloe.

"He could be dangerous."

Muldoon left them in Chloe's room to figure out for themselves what they would do with that request, and, grabbing Lacey from a peephole outside of Chloe's room, headed back to the bridewell.

"I am innocent," John Bryant said, resting his cuffed hands on his lap. Wilcox sat beside him, waiting to offer counsel if John required it.

"That may reveal itself to be the case, Mr Bryant, but we still have a murder on our hands. You must know something." Gill took a deep breath. "So let's start again. When did you secure the deeds to five Percy Street?"

"May of this year. 1892," Bryant said.

"Do you have the papers for that?"

"I did," he said. "Mr Ellman sold the house to me. It had been his, and he had no use for it as he lived in a mansion out in the countryside. It came as part of the employment contract. I had my own copies."

Gill jutted his chin forward in thought. "I must say, Mr Bryant, it's quite unusual for a man as wealthy as yourself to need an *employer* after that stint in Australia. You must be rolling in it, if you'll beg my pardon for such a crude expression."

Bryant shrugged. "He was very convincing, and I wanted to give the girls a good life—that is, my wife and daughter. Look—at the end of the day, I'm still just a sheep farmer. I didn't think anything of it, working for him. I thought that's what you do, so I took everything he offered. He was so nice to me... Cared about my life and my dreams, you know?"

Muldoon nodded sympathetically. "And you have no idea where those papers are?"

"No. I brought them with me to Percy street. They must be in the house somewhere?"

"We've searched the premises several times," Muldoon said regretfully. "Our officers can't find anything."

"Well, look again! I signed the contract *on the ship* and as soon as the ship docked, I went to see it with him. He'd just had it all decorated and he suggested I went shopping and had it outfitted, which I did." Bryant smacked his lips together. "It was too good to be true."

"So you have no idea who the woman in the attic is?"

Bryant shook his head. Wilcox cleared his throat and said, "as I have previously stated, Chief Inspector Gill, my client has no connection whatsoever to Mary Hobbs."

Gill folded his arms and frowned. "You might not, but you're still involved in this, somehow, Bryant, and I'm going to find out how."

28

Mary looked up at the pale light filtering in through the bricked up windows, and held her knees closer to her chest. Her chamber pot, full and foul-smelling, rested by the door. She shivered uncontrollably as the fever soaked her blood-stained dress. She closed her eyes and imagined what her loved ones were doing right at that moment. She tried to visualise their faces, but her daydream was interrupted by the knocking on the door.

"Mary, do you want to come out?" The sound of his voice made the hairs on the back of her neck stand erect.

"No," she said, trembling.

"Don't be ridiculous, Mary. Just tell me and I'll let you out. I'll even get you a doctor."

"No," she said again. "It's a trick."

"Mary," he said, "why must you torment me like this? You can come out."

She ran her hands down her body to her abdomen, which was still soft and swollen, but its emptiness further highlighted how alone she was now. "No. You will hurt me."

"I would never hurt you, Mary, as long as you don't misbehave. Unfortunately, you have misbehaved, and for that you must be punished."

She thought of the life that was no longer inside of her, and with a broken voice, said, "I am punished enough." She broke into a sob.

"Maggie is here, Mary."

Mary gasped and held her breath.

"Yes," he continued softly. "Maggie is right here, and she can help you."

"You're lying!" she cried, trembling again as beads of sweat rolled down her forehead. Her lips, cracked and in desperate need of water, parted again to take another deep breath. She licked the salty tears as they stung the sores around her mouth.

"Mary?" she heard a woman's voice ask.

"Maggie? Oh Maggie! Is that you?" Her tears merged with the dirt and blood on her face as she brushed them across her cheeks like warpaint. There was a thud and he returned to the door.

"See, I brought Maggie to see you. Now come out. The sooner you face your punishment, the sooner we can be happy again."

She heard Maggie whimpering somewhere on the other side of the door. "Please don't hurt her! Please." Mary heard the crack of a belt as it made contact with what she presumed was Maggie's skin, as her shrieks and sobs followed soon after. "Please. Stop it!" Mary screamed, covering her ears. "Stop it!"

"If it bothers you so much, Mary, you should do the hon-
ourable thing... and come and take her place!"

"Well that puts a cat amongst the pigeons," Gill snarled, lighting
his pipe. They looked down at the dead body on the table.
Muldoon studied the gash on Maggie's neck, and looked across
to the razor that rested on the trolley. It was the same style as the
one found under Mrs Mckinnon's bed, but it did not belong to
John Bryant.

As Bryant's bags were held in the storeroom of the bridewell
while he was detained, Muldoon took it upon himself to search
through the suspect's belongings. The razors that he found bore
the inscription *Hargreaves, Smith & Co SHEFFIELD* on the
smooth, steel face of the blade. The faces of the two razors found
in the house were *Milton & Sons, SHEFFIELD*.

"I suppose we'll have to let Bryant go then." Gill puffed at the
pipe for a minute and muttered, "bugger. Any family we need
to notify?"

"A sister," said Muldoon. "In Allerton."

"Have someone write to her. Let her know she needs to come
and identify the body. How's Mrs Mckinnon?"

Muldoon brought Mrs Mckinnon a cup of tea in Gill's office.
"I'd just gone out for some things," she said with a trembling
bottom lip. Gill cast his eyes downward and waited for her to
compose herself. "I was gone for half an hour, no more. Just

to get some more soap... more soap for me and Maggie. When I left her, she was cleaning the grate, you know, as the Bryants weren't around and we didn't need to have it lit... I popped out for some more soap and..." Violet Mckinnon held her chin in her hand as the first tears gently ran from her eyes. "And then she was dead. Just like that? It was only Maggie and myself in there. I only went out for soap!" Mrs Mckinnon broke into a sob and shook her head. "I'm sorry," she said, sniffing and wiping her tears away. "It's all such a shock."

"Is there anyone who may have wanted to hurt Maggie, Mrs Mckinnon?"

"No!" She dabbed the wet patches on her cheeks with her handkerchief and continued, admirably. "As far as I knew, she didn't have anybody. She certainly never mentioned anyone, but then, she hardly spoke!"

Fred Wilcox, despite not having his services required any more, was more than happy to assist Muldoon with his investigation. Muldoon, sure that the secretary would have recognised him, or been alarmed at the sight of a uniformed constable, asked Wilcox to 'get a feel for Ellman's diary this week,' and pretend to be a salesman. Wilcox was successful, and managed to find out that Ellman was in his offices all week. Rather than write to Cecilia Ross, they decided to take a train to Allerton and see her personally, during the hours that Ellman would not be there.

They were not granted an audience with Miss Ross because the gatekeeper had allowed them to come in, but because Paulie McCrae had been flung over the wall first, sneaking around the back in search of the lady with the dog. When he found her, she followed him to the gate, the magic word to win her cooperation being no other than the name of her sister: Maggie.

"I always knew this would happen," she said, her shoulders sinking. Muldoon took note of how angry the young woman was.

"Do you know who might have done this, Miss Ross?"

"I do." She lifted her sad, blue eyes and looked at him. "It was my brother."

Wilcox and Muldoon looked at one another. Muldoon tilted his head and said, "your brother, Miss Ross?"

"My surname isn't actually Ross. Rather, it was my mother's family name. My name—and Maggie's name, is Ellman."

Fred almost choked on his tea, hearing the revelation. "Maggie is Thomas Ellman's daughter?" asked Muldoon, remaining calm. Margaret Ross' letters had briefly mentioned her father, after all. "And you too, are his daughter?"

"Yes. From his second marriage. Maggie and I are twins, in case it wasn't apparent." She flashed a brief smile, and returned to her deep thoughts. "My father loves us, you see, but he doesn't love all of his children equally... Teddy—Edward Thomas Ellman—is a cruel man, and had been a wicked, unnatural child. I would put my inheritance on him being the killer. Ever since we were small, he has despised us and controlled us. When father would go away on business, he would lock us in the cupboard for hours. Once, we were in there for two days, with my mother worrying sick at being unable to find us. You see, he told us not to make a sound, or he'd drown our kittens in the well, or cut our hair off, or whatever cruel threat he could think of. On many occasions, we would come out of a cupboard, a wardrobe, or a crawlspace crying and soaked in our own filth. Mother would try and tell father but he simply laughed and said Teddy was just teasing us, and that boys will be boys.

His torment only grew worse over the years. He would cut our skin, torture our pets..." she brought the spaniel in her arms closer to her face and cuddled it, "and have us offer ourselves up in their places if it was bothering us." She let the little dog jump off her lap, pulled her collar down and revealed a long scar on her neck that ran down to her collarbone. "Father wouldn't believe me, so I stopped trying. Maggie stopped trying, but she resisted his cruelty for the longest. She despised them both, in the end. I learned quite soon that if you just did as Teddy said, you would be left alone, and father wouldn't be so angry with you for telling tales.

One day, when we were fourteen, we found our mother's body at the foot of the stairs. Her neck was broken. I'll never forget it. It was him. She got in the way of father's affections and by extension—so did we. My father hasn't been the same since. He is still mourning her death, which was almost ten years ago now."

Wilcox listened, horrified. "Miss Ross, why did you not inform the police?"

She shook her head, her top lip curling into a sneer. "When your father is as rich and powerful as mine, who would believe me? Besides, I depend on him for a roof over my head and food in my belly. Such is the curse of a woman of my class. I am property."

Muldoon reached for the photograph of Mary and laid it on the table. Cecilia stared at it, letting the tears roll down her rosy cheeks, each one splashing onto her lap.

"Who is Mary?" Muldoon asked quietly, "and why did she write you so often before her murder?"

"Mary was our friend." She wiped the tears away with the back of her petite hands. "She was a dear friend. Her parents, the Hobbs's, live only a mile west of us, and we were good friends growing up. When she was sixteen, she became besotted with Teddy and by eighteen, she was gone."

Muldoon picked up his cup of tea. "We found letters that she'd written."

"Then you will know that she feared for her life. She told us everything, when she had the chance. Maggie found her eventually, living in Percy Street, but once you've stepped into the spider's web, you can't get out."

Frances Bryant's ramblings came to mind. *He is the spider; we are the flies.* He swallowed. "What do you mean?" he asked.

"He wouldn't let her leave. He kept her there to help him..." As strong as Cecilia's reserve had seemed, holding back more tears became too much of a challenge. She couldn't keep them at bay forever. "When... when Mary was murdered... father told Maggie to keep it a secret, and not to tell a soul. If she did, he would strip both of us of everything we had and turn us out. You see, our mother didn't have much. She had been the housekeeper when he was married to Teddy's mother. When Mrs Ellman died, my mother was a source of comfort for my father. Their marriage was a happy one... most of the time, but because mother had no wealth of her own, their marriage rendered us completely dependent on him and by extension, Teddy. Had either Maggie or I had the good fortune to have been born a boy, I believe with all my heart that Teddy would be rotting away in an asylum, and father would have given us the world." She smiled, despite her tears. "Do you believe in karma, gentlemen?"

"I know of it. I have friends in India," Wilcox said. "It's Hindu, I think, is it not?"

She smiled and nodded gracefully. "My brother is a murderer, and he is cruel. He is the favoured one, but his name will fade into obscurity. With any luck, you'll have him hanged, and his wealth will pass to my niece."

"Your niece?" Muldoon asked.

"Yes," Cecilia nodded. "Mary, during her marriage, bore that monster a child."

The two men looked at each other. Muldoon turned his face back to Cecilia and asked, "Where is the child now?"

Cecilia looked about the room nervously and lowered her voice. "The child is with her mother's family. Teddy thinks that Mary had a stillborn and hid it from him. This was the only way we could think of that wouldn't result in him hunting his heir down. Maggie left her in a basket for me to collect at the hotel she used to send me letters from. I took her back to her grandparents, and asked them to arrange for a wet nurse for the poor, hungry thing. This was what Mary wanted, and she had attached a note for them to read, so they knew it was genuine. They asked no questions, and raised no alarm, for they knew. They knew that Mary's life was in danger." Cecilia wiped away more tears. "And he killed her anyway. After all that." Cecilia looked up at the ceiling and back to her inquisitors, resolute. "That little girl will never know of what her father did, if I can help it."

"Does your father know about the child?"

Cecilia shook her head. "Absolutely not."

"Do you know where your brother is?"

"No, and that is what vexes me." She gave a wry smile. "I would help you push him off the nearest cliff, if I could find him."

"Miss Ross," Muldoon said, pulling Sarah's sketch out of his pocket and unfolding it onto the table. "Is this your brother?"

She nodded slowly, and said, "that's certainly his likeness. I haven't seen him for some time, but that is him."

29

"There's someone watching that house around the clock. If Edward Ellman has access to Percy Street, he'll have a hard time getting past the front gate," Gill said to Lacey. "It's your watch at eight o'clock tomorrow. Go home and get some rest."

Lacey left Gill with Mrs Mckinnon and John Bryant outside the main entrance of the bridewell, where a cab driver was strapping their bags to the back of the vehicle.

"Well, I suppose that's it for now then," Gill said, shaking Bryant's hand. "You've been put through the mangle."

John Bryant half-laughed, and looked up at the bridewell. "Glad to be on this side of the wall again."

"We'll be in touch when we have more information on your case."

Bryant looked at Gill and frowned. "He would have had me sent to the gallows." He looked down at his shoes and shook his head. "I don't know how someone could do that."

"You'd be amazed, Mr Bryant," Gill said, placing a cigar in the breast pocket of Bryant's jacket. "Take care."

John Bryant thanked him and waited beside the cab as Mrs Mckinnon turned to speak to Gill.

"I need to take care of the poor man, and I'm sure there are some people over the water desperate to see him," Violet Mckinnon said, shaking Gill's hand.

Much to Gill's delight, Violet Mckinnon was as sweet and as kind as she had appeared to be, and she had made a comment about what an excellent cup of tea he made in spite of being *such a busy and hard-working man*.

"I hope you find whoever did this, Mr Gill," she said. "That girl... she didn't deserve that."

"I know, Mrs Mckinnon. We're doing all we can."

The old lady looked up at his grave face and smiled faintly. "Well, goodbye then," she said, pulling her shawl closer to her neck.

"Safe journey, Mrs Mckinnon."

Gill waved farewell to Mrs Mckinnon and John Bryant as they climbed into the cab. After the driver closed the door, Gill instructed the man to take them to the ferry terminal. The driver stirred the bay horses into action, and Gill watched the animals gracefully pull away, their heads bobbing rhythmically to the clip-clop of their hooves. One turn around the corner and they were gone.

Gill stood for a moment and watched the late afternoon sunset descending onto the rooftops, casting its pink halo around their sharp-angled silhouettes. Anger and frustration bubbled in his gut.

"Well, Mulders, what now then?" he asked, looking straight ahead.

"How did you—?"

Gill smiled and turned around to look at Muldoon. "I've come to expect you lurking there in the shadows, my friend."

"Thomas Ellman is under house arrest, as you asked. He knows why, but he won't talk."

"Twat."

"Indeed, Gov."

"How's the girl?"

Cecilia had made them promise not to say a word. She assured them that the servants felt no loyalty to their master, and could be persuaded to support her in a time of need. "They've witnessed every horror this family has endured. They are as helpless as I am," she said as she bade them farewell. There was no telling how the trial would go when Ellman had the money to guarantee witness intimidation and the cover up that would follow, but Gill was trying to be optimistic.

"She'll be all right," Muldoon said. "Her father doesn't know we've spoken to her, and she's devastated about her sister. She'll testify against both of them in court. We've got a stack of evidence on him as high as that wall," Muldoon said, indicating at the severe, brick walls surrounding the fortress that was The Main Bridewell. "We've got Thomas Ellman for forgery, blackmail, bribery, and now he's an accomplice in not one but two murders. He was happy to have John Bryant fitted up for his son's crimes, and would have let us hang the poor bastard."

"We'll go and speak to him tomorrow, and we'll meet his army of solicitors, no doubt." Gill placed his hands in his pockets and walked closer to Muldoon. "I'd say let's go for a drink but, I don't think it'll do anything to take away the bitter taste of defeat. I have sent a warrant out though, for Edward Ellman. Not sure what use that would be, when no one's seen him for ages."

"I know someone who's seen him," Muldoon said.

"A drawing doesn't count, Mulders."

"She must have seen him though. He's been in the house. He stole her drawers for Christ's sake."

"He hasn't come back to Madame Chloe?"

Muldoon shook his head. "No. They're shit scared of him now, so they'd definitely tell me if he does."

"What to do then?" Gill sighed.

"We could take another look at the crime scene?"

Gill frowned. "Yes, right. That's what you do for fun, isn't it Mulders?"

"I won't sleep 'til this is solved, Gov. Might as well be productive."

They approached number five at sunset with a lantern and a bag of tools. Robertson was stationed on the doorstep when they arrived, but Gill offered him a leg stretch. He took it without hesitation, and assured them he'd be in earshot if they needed him.

The street was eerily quiet in the crisp November twilight. In the fading light, Muldoon lifted his lantern so Gill could see the lock. He fished for a key in his pocket and finding the right one, unlocked it. They entered the silent, empty house and closed the door behind them. "Well then," Gill said, putting the key back in his pocket. "You got your whistle, just in case?"

Muldoon nodded and put the lantern on the sideboard in the hallway. It cast a ghostly glow around the area, highlighting the shadowed fingers of the parlour palm as they stretched out in every direction. In the gloom, he retrieved his match box. He took a moment to light some of the lamps in the hallway and the parlour room: the focal point of the decor now being a chalk outline of where Maggie's body had lain.

"Is it still haunted then?" asked Gill quietly. "Is the maid here with us?"

Muldoon looked at him and, seeing that he was uneasy, shook his head. "Not that I can sense."

Gill grunted and lifted the lantern over the outline. "Right then..."

They were silent for a moment, and studied the room. Muldoon crouched down to get closer to the outline, and turned to follow the trail of broken pottery. He stood up and went to the windowsill. The little figurine, after all of the near misses, had finally succumbed to gravity, and lay smashed. He placed the larger of the pieces back on the ledge.

"Was the back door locked on the morning of the murder?" he asked.

"Yeah. That's what Pinners said, anyway. No signs of forced entry. Mrs Mckinnon left for the shops through the front."

"The struggle was here, and this is no doubt where it happened," Muldoon said.

Even in the low light, the discoloration on the floor where Maggie spent her final seconds on earth represented the legacy of suffering: a permanent stain on the soul of the house. He imagined her wide eyes, looking helplessly at him through the window, where he couldn't see her or do anything to help. *I'm sorry, Maggie.*

"So I have a theory, Gov," Muldoon began. "Poor Maggie here, held against her will, had to do as she was told. What if the deeds—the real deeds—were stashed away?"

Gill cocked his head, listening. "What, like, in the floorboards?"

"Is that where you'd hide them?"

"Either that or I'd burn 'em."

"If you absolutely despised the men who were making you get rid of them, would you destroy them or just hide them in the hope they could be used as evidence one day?"

"I'd lose my rag and burn them," Gill admitted.

Muldoon laughed and shook his head. "Think like a woman, Gov," he said. "Hell hath no fury like a woman scorned. Get in her mind, Gov—what would you do?"

He pursed his lips for a moment in deep thought, and said, "I'd cry about it for a bit... then I'd stash it away."

"It's not going to take long, is it? This house is... unsettling," Gill said as Muldoon rooted through the toolbag.

"Big Bad Police Chief is scared of a haunted house, I see."

"Piss off, you know what I mean."

Muldoon smirked and handed Gill a crowbar.

They set to work in Maggie's room first. "I hope Bryant doesn't mind us ripping up his walls and floors." Gill said, pushing the crowbar into the slats. "Nice wood, this. Varnished and all, even down here." The wood groaned and creaked as Gill pulled the boards from the beams underneath. "Does make me wonder, Mulders," Gill mused. "How did the bastard get in?"

Hours passed as they moved piece after piece, working into the night. "Oi," Gill said, wiping some sweat from his brow. "Reckon they've got supplies in for us to make a cuppa?"

"They might," Muldoon shrugged. "You go ahead, I think I'm nearly done here."

Gill left him alone to push the bed out of the way and dig down into the floor. His fingertips touched something of interest, forcing him to stretch his arm even further to the point where he felt it would come out of its socket. He clumsily clutched the corner of paper—his fingertips like pincers, and he gently pulled. In the dim light, he brushed some dust off the documents. They were the deeds for the house, and more.

Hearing a thud and a crash upstairs, he quickly folded the documents, stuffing them into his inside pocket. "Gov?" he called. Gill didn't respond, and the basement door slammed shut. "Gov, what's going on?"

Muldoon, crowbar in hand, ran up the steps and tried the brass doorknob. Locked. He rattled it desperately. "Gov?" The crashes and the sounds of a struggle continued. "Gov?" Muldoon lunged at the door, smashing down on the knob with his crowbar. Blow by blow, he beat it until it sprang from the door, taking splinters of wood with it. He gave the door one more shove with his foot and broke out of the basement.

Panting, he peered out into the hallway. Not even the grandfather clock ticked any more. He crept towards the corridor leading to the back kitchen. Hearing another struggle characterised by the crash of pots and pans and Gill shouting something, he ran into the kitchen.

He found Gill lying in a pool of his own blood, clutching at a wound on his shoulder. In response, Muldoon's own blood ran cold. He knelt down and assessed the damage. "What? What with?" he asked. Gill nodded at something behind him. There was a bloodied screwdriver on the tiled floor.

"Get the bastard," Gill whispered. Muldoon rose from the floor and ran to the front door, opened it, and blew his whistle with fury.

Robertson was the first to arrive on the scene. Deciding that there wouldn't be enough time to get Gill to a surgeon if they waited for a wagon, he threw the Chief Inspector's good arm over his shoulders and bore his weight as they headed to the cab rank to flag a driver down.

Muldoon couldn't wait any longer for reinforcements. The adrenaline rushing through his limbs compelled him to lock the front door, pick up a hammer and hunt the killer down.

He returned to the kitchen where he had to step over the drying pool of Gill's blood. He looked up at the washing line: men's shirts. He stepped forward and parted them, revealing nothing but a bare wall. Turning around, he tried the back door, but it was boarded up. He looked out into the corridor joining the kitchen to the hallway and heard nothing.

Returning to the kitchen, he raised his hammer in anticipation. "Where are you?" he asked, looking around the walls and up at the ceiling. His eyes stopped when he saw Maggie standing in the kitchen doorway. Her eyes, dead and frightened like Mary's had been, lifted over him and focused on the wall behind him. She raised her hand and pointed. Without requiring any further explanation, Muldoon swung the hammer over his head. Plaster crumbled all over the floor, its dust floating into his nostrils and throat. He hammered again, finding more force to throw it with each time. Bricks gave way and he pulled them out with his bare hands to find a narrow gap between an interior wall and exterior wall. He looked closely: there was enough room for a man to have stood there and breathed comfortably. He held his breath, listening. Somewhere in the walls, he could hear shuffling. He followed the sound with his hands and stopped at a picture hanging on the wall beside a Welsh dresser. He removed it, and met the eyes of his prey. Before Muldoon could blink, the eyes disappeared, and he threw his hammer at the wall again. Reaching in, he found nothing. He bent down to the dresser and opened a cupboard door. As with the wardrobe in the nursery, the back panel had been moved aside and exposed the cavity of the interior wall behind it, but it was too late for Muldoon to climb in. The assailant had moved on. The sound of something rubbing against the wall left the kitchen, and he heard footsteps out in the hall, scurrying away like a rat. He turned to look at the doorway, and found Maggie still standing there. She turned her body away and, checking to see that he was still looking, gestured for him to follow.

Muldoon silently followed the apparition as she led him to the hallway, stopping outside the drawing room. She placed her finger to her lips as he heard a "shh" wash over him. It seemed to come from every room, echoing in his ears. The front door was locked. There was nowhere for Teddy Ellman to go. He followed the direction of where she had turned her face and slowly crept into the drawing room.

He waited.

The chalk outline of Maggie's body caught his eye as he tried to process what her ghost was showing him. He entered, and turned to see Mary in the corner of the room, but for once, she wasn't looking at him. Expressionless, she stood pointing at the hearth.

Without any further thought, Muldoon crept toward the black, unlit hearth and crouched down to look inside. For a moment, he was staring into a black abyss, until he could make out the whites of a man's eyes. Lunging with both hands into the shadows, he grabbed the collar of a shirt. With a loud rip, it tore as the object of his pursuit pulled away and tried to clamber up the chimney. Muldoon lunged again and grabbed a bony ankle, ripping Ellman from the chimney with all of his strength. He threw the murderer onto the parlour room floor. Clouds of soot blackened the nearby upholstery as the pursuit came to a climax. Ellman, like a wounded animal, rolled around the floor and groaned as Muldoon furiously kicked him and pinned him in place. Ellman was thin, and covered in soot, but Muldoon knew that the eyes staring at him now had been the last that Mary Hobbs and Margaret Ross had seen.

30

Wilcox and Muldoon stood outside the sunroom of Springheath Hall, awaiting the meeting that Ellman had requested the day before. "There's nothing he can deny," Wilcox began quietly. "The man had something on absolutely every accomplice; Jessops would do anything to disguise his secret preference for male company, Swinson and his fear of anyone exposing his secret family... the list just goes on." Fred shook his head. "I'd be amazed if there was anything to talk about this morning."

Thomas Edward Ellman sat in his sunroom, wearing his smoking jacket as though nothing had happened in the last twenty-four hours. Only, something had happened. He looked wan, lifting his eyes to look at Muldoon as though it caused him immense strain in the grey morning light.

"Just us, chaps," he said with a slight slurring of his speech. Fumes of brandy sailed into the air, riding on his breath. "Let's get on with it."

"Mr Ellman," Muldoon began, "are you saying you're *not* seeking counsel?"

The old man seemed exhausted, staring at them with heavy bags under his eyes. "That is exactly what I am saying," he said in a low growl.

Muldoon looked at Wilcox and then back at the old man. "Why the change of heart, Mr Ellman?"

"It's not a change of heart. It's rather a case of what I deserve," he said, glancing over their heads for a second. "I made the wrong choices. I am responsible for the murders, even if I didn't commit them myself. 'If we confess our sins, he is faithful and just to forgive us our sins and to cleanse us from all unright-eousness' and it is therefore what I should do."

"It is not that you are directly responsible for your son's actions—"

"But I am!" he cried, slamming his fist down on the table. "I lost a daughter, because I loved my son too much. One man cannot serve two masters, and I served him and myself. I am ashamed of what I've done."

"Did you ever suspect that your son had some involvement in your second wife's death?"

He nodded. "I denied it to myself, because I wanted to believe otherwise." He hung his head for a moment, and when he raised it again, he said with a breaking voice, "what are you supposed to do when you discover that your son—even as a child—is a monster? Long has it been since the days when you could leave deformed children on the mountainside to die. If I was to send him away... I couldn't. I couldn't do it. My love for him clouded my judgement, and now I have lost two children." He snorted, and followed with, "I suspect that Cecilia will never speak to me again, so let's make that three. The things that..." he sniffed and tried to hold back tears. "The things I made that girl do... just to save... I am the monster." He jabbed himself in the chest repeatedly with his finger. "I let Maggie down. I let my girls down. I am the monster."

"Mr Ellman, I have the confessions for you to sign," Muldoon said, gently. "First, we need your confession to orchestrating the poisoning of Frances Bryant, the blackmail of Dr Edward Swinson and of Michael Jessops. We need you to confess to forgery concerning John Bryant, and for perverting the course of justice on five counts." Fred laid the documents out in a pile in front of Ellman, who took a deep breath and dipped his steel pen into the inkwell on the table. Muldoon and Wilcox watched him sign each one, as though it had been a pile of business contracts and he wanted to hurry up and finish for the day.

"Perverting the course of justice. That's a new one, I take it?" He blew the last line of ink and pushed the papers back at Wilcox.

"Quite recent, yes. Long overdue, as well, in my opinion," Wilcox said with an awkward smile.

Ellman sat there for a moment and stared into space. "So what now then?"

"Prison, Mr Ellman," Muldoon replied. "You'll be tried for these crimes and likely sentenced to life imprisonment... but of course, that's up to the judge."

"Very well," he said, swallowing. "My will is written. Cecilia gets everything. Every last penny, every last brick. It is the least I can do…" He smiled through what looked like the first crash of his bottom lip and took another deep breath. "Now, gentlemen. May I have a moment alone before I accompany you back to Liverpool?"

Wilcox left the room first. Muldoon, just as he had turned out of the doorway, remembered something, and turned around. When he re-entered the room to collect his hat, he was met with Ellman holding a pistol to his head.

Muldoon stood in the doorway, saying nothing. Their eyes met. Ellman's were wide, bloodshot and desperate: Muldoon's, emotionless and steady. The seconds that passed felt like hours, as Ellman's hand shook violently, pushing the slender barrel to his temple. "Let me die alone," Ellman pleaded, with quick breaths. Muldoon opened his mouth, but couldn't find the words. "Afford me this quiet death," the man said through gritted teeth.

Cecilia appeared in the room, her skirts brushing against the door frame as she slid past Muldoon. Red-faced, Ellman began to cry. "No! You cannot see me like this!" he yelled.

She shook her head calmly, and slowly approached the table. With a fair, pixie-like hand, she wrapped her fingers around the handle of the gun and steadily lowered it from his head without a word. She then took the weapon from his hands and dropped it on the floor, and collapsed into her father's lap, sobbing.

"I am not worthy," he said, stroking her soft hair as she released fresh tears into the fabric of his smoking jacket.

"If I can find it in my heart to forgive you, father," she said as she wept, and looked up at him, "then you can listen to me as I tell you this now." She wiped away her tears and stared into his eyes as she held his face in her hands. "I believe in all that is just and fair in this world, and I know that deep down…" she steadied her whimpering and continued, "you do, too. And that is why you must go now. You must do this the right way. You, father, can still be a decent man, and you know that you must do the right thing."

Father looked at daughter as though he was seeing her for the first time. Muldoon silently turned away, leaving them to say their final farewell in private.

Margaret Emily Ross Ellman and Mary Elizabeth Hobbs were buried side by side in St James' cemetery the following week. Edward Ellman, remorseless and—thanks to his father—without representation, was sentenced to be hanged on the morning of December 18th, 1892. The scandal caused much hubbub among the mourners and their respective staff and tenants, as well as the wider population. Breakfast tables across the region found themselves plastered with front page stories about 'Teddy Ellman, *The Spider* who haunted a family at number five'. Both Ellman men covered the front covers for weeks, bringing hundreds to huddle in coffee houses and tearooms to hear the latest about the killer who lived in the walls of Percy Street, waiting to trap his next victim.

"It just doesn't bear thinking about," Sarah said, covering herself with her cape as a small burst of sleet descended on the mourners.

"I wouldn't have found him if it wasn't for your drawing," Muldoon said. She blushed.

"I didn't know... I drew something from a dream I'd had. I didn't realise that he... it sickens me."

"I'm sorry that I didn't take your allegation seriously," he said.

"It's no matter. It was the strangest thing, and I knew it must have sounded ridiculous."

"That's the last time I'll ever doubt a woman," Muldoon said.

She smiled at him, and said, "you're a wise man, Inspector."

"Please," he said. "Call me Daniel."

Muldoon stood with Fred Wilcox and the Bryants at the back of the dense swarm of mourners. "I wanted to say goodbye," Frances said. "I didn't know either of them particularly, but we are a part of each other's lives now, in one way or another. I can't bear to think of the suffering they had to endure."

From where they stood, they could see the Hobbs family standing at the graveside, as well as Cecilia Ellman and her four-year-old niece, Polly. The little girl was wearing the gold necklace that had once belonged to her mother. Muldoon had the necklace cleaned, polished and returned to the family. "Why didn't you just have her buried with it?" Gill asked, wondering why anyone would want the necklace found on a murder victim.

"Mary wanted me to give it to them," he said. "And I value my sleep."

Gill, understanding that the mysterious ways in which Muldoon had to work, were not worth questioning, nodded. His wound was healing faster than expected, but he was instructed to stay home and rest. Ablewhite prescribed fresh air, good food and 'no police business.'

Muldoon, catching sight of Mary and Maggie, held his breath. They were dressed smartly, and if he hadn't known otherwise, seemed alive. They waved and smiled as they looked at each other and back to him. Mary had her hand on the little girl's shoulder, and Maggie stood beside her twin, who was wiping away tears. Muldoon turned to Frances, who had seen them too. When they looked up at the grave again, the ghosts had gone.

Long after the mourners had parted ways and vacated the cemetery, Muldoon accompanied the Bryant family back to Percy street where a couple of carters were loading their belongings onto a covered wagon.

"You're leaving?" Muldoon asked.

"Yes," John Bryant said. "Too much has happened here."

"Where will you go?" Muldoon's eyes met with Sarah's.

John looked up at the house. "We are set up with some apartments in Chester for now, and then I was thinking of buying a farm." He turned to his wife and smiled, reaching for her hand. "Life was simpler then, wasn't it?"

"It was," she agreed, holding his hand tightly. Frances was still thin, but the light had returned to her eyes. "And even though he's gone... I couldn't sleep at night knowing he had lived right there with us, hiding in the walls. It is a horror that will stay with me for a long time, but we must look to the future and be glad that he's gone." She shook her head, sending her pearl drop earrings swinging, and looked back at Muldoon. "Inspector, forgive me if this is forward but, we were wondering..." she looked at Sarah for a second. "We were wondering if you would like to come and spend Christmas with us... that is, if you don't have any other plans? Mrs Mckinnon has made a rather large Christmas pudding, you see..."

Muldoon, taken aback, smiled. "What a generous offer," he said. He looked at Sarah Jones, who blushed and cast her round, silk-lidded eyes at the floor. "I don't have any other offers, and I am owed some time off after all... I'd be more than happy to come and visit for Christmas."

"The little boy can come, too, of course," Frances added.

"Thank you. Paulie will be thrilled. You are too kind."

John held out a hand. "It's the least we could do, after everything you've done for us." The two men shook hands. "Our train leaves in two hours, so we'd better get on. Here." Bryant pulled a slip of paper out of his pocket and handed it to Muldoon. "That's where to find us."

"Have a safe journey," Muldoon said, placing the paper in his breast pocket. The Bryants went back into the house to collect their final things and wait for the cab, leaving Muldoon and Sarah alone beside the wagon.

"You look flushed, Miss Jones," he said.

Her eyes widened, and she looked away shyly. "Please, we are beyond that now. You can call me Sarah, and you didn't have to say 'yes' out of politeness... I'm sorry that Frances has taken it upon herself to play matchmaker."

"I'm not."

She relaxed her shoulders and laughed with relief. "So now that that's settled," she said, looking at the house and then back at the inspector. "I look forward to getting to know you, Daniel."

"Goodbye for now, then, Sarah Jones."

"Goodbye," she said, entering through the gate and turning to look at him once more with a smile.

Muldoon tipped his hat, turned on his heel and headed west toward the fading sun.

December 18th, 1892

Dear Margaret,

This morning, I awoke before the rest of the household in a manner similar to Christmas morning. The air was cold, but my mind was on the gallows. I am confused by my own feelings of delight on such a monumental day as this. Even in the darkest depths, even when our souls are shadowed by evil that seeks to break us, there is magic in the world, and I found it this morning. The frost sparkled on every blade of grass I happened to look upon, and I savoured every moment that I spent crossing the lawn to wait for the church bells to ring. A little robin came to sit beside me for a time, until Fig chased it away with his yapping. On the eighth bell, I collapsed onto the ground and wept with relief. He is dead.

The justice that he has been served will not bring you back to me. I know this. But I also know that somewhere, you can hear me.

Your death was not in vain. That little girl is alive because of you. She is growing more like Mary each and every day, and you will live in her life just as I do. Mr and Mrs Hobbs have invited me to stay with them. At first, I thought they meant just for Christmas, but they knew of my situation, and wished for me to stay with them indefinitely, if I should be unable to find more suitable lodgings. That is very kind of them, and I shall certainly consider it. I love that child with a fervour akin to what her own mother would have bestowed upon her. She will only know love.

Father is in prison, as he should be. I'm afraid I shall never see him again. As he had no living sons, the business passed on to me when he was sentenced, and I aim to sell the lot. Nothing will remain of Ellman and Co. and I have more than enough to have a long and happy life. I dread to think of what he did with that wealth. I learned of Mr Bryant's treatment, and it horrified me, so I sent the family thirty gold sovereigns, as compensation, and they shall have the fattest goose for Christmas. I hope that that will be enough.

My love, always,

Sissy.

Epilogue

The deep grey clouds, pregnant with the swell of snow, hovered over the city as Father Brown finished dressing and prepared to emerge from his quarters. Heavy and aching, his head throbbed as he tried to drink some water; it was no use, and resulted in him leaning over the basin, trying not to retch.

His hands felt cold to the bone as he rubbed them together over the small fire. He winced as something under his shirt dug into his neck with a sting, but in his stoicity, he chose to ignore it. Still wearing his blanket over his head, he left his bedroom and passed his housekeeper in the passage that connected the rectory to the church. "Good morning, Father," she said, busily sweeping up in the corridor. It was eleven o'clock, and Father Brown, usually a master at timekeeping, was late for confession.

"Morning, Mrs Flaherty," he said, suddenly conscious of the way he might have looked with a blanket around his head.

She eyed the blanket and smiled knowingly. "It's a bit cold this morning, Father. Are you well?"

He stopped for a moment, and pondered. "Perfectly fine, thanks," he said, eyeing her full bosom and fat, round hips under her apron. Glistening with light perspiration, her skin, pink and full of life, distracted him from the conversation. For a moment, she didn't notice as she swept, until she caught him still standing there in the corner of her eye.

Mrs Flaherty, thwarted by her arthritis in cold weather, stopped what she was doing and stood upright, leaning on the broom handle. She stared at him peculiarly. "Are you sure you don't need some broth or a cup of tea?" she asked, concerned. What little grey light there was, shone through the rooms, leaving the corridor in shadow. She couldn't read his expression, but noticed how the glow in his cheeks and twinkling of his eyes gave the impression of fever. It was winter, after all.

"No thank you, Mrs Flaherty. I'm... I'm fasting today," he said, swallowing the saliva as it coated his teeth.

"Very well," she said, observing his gaunt, hungry features that adorned his smooth, porcelain visage. "There are some people already waiting for confession, Father," she said. "So I'll let you get on." She began to hum and continued with her work, leaving him to shuffle down the darkened corridor in peace.

Muldoon waited in the confession box and relaxed when he heard the priest climb in and sit down.

"Forgive me Father, but I am about to sin."

There was a prolonged silence, followed by the rustling of a vestment. "How so?" the priest finally asked.

Muldoon, overpowered by the stench of death, looked up and covered his mouth with a handkerchief. The confession box was soaked in it: decaying, flesh-ridden death and despair.

"See, Father... I followed a breadcrumb trail—only—the bread-crumbs were bodies. Bodies of women, children...of choir boys. You're careless, and you're messy, and you're going to have to die, Father."

"What are you talking about?"

"It's a miracle, really. Here we are, slowly approaching the middle of the day, and I'd expect to see a pile of ashes there where you're sitting right now, what with all the crucifixes but... anyway, any final words?"

"Disease!" he cried. "It was disease! It's winter! I was giving them their last rites."

He heard the priest fiddling with the door on the other side of the box. "It's no use, Father. It's locked from the outside." Muldoon looked down at his lap. "Last night, while you were out hunting, the top of this box was removed and replaced with a sheet. In a moment, I'll be pulling that cover off the top of the box, and the sun will deliver swift justice."

"What is this? Let me out right now! Right now or I shall be calling for the police."

Muldoon lowered his head, and smirked.

Closing the rattling confession box with a respectful turn of the handle, Muldoon nodded to Lacey, who helped him pull the thick cover from the top of the tall mahogany structure. The late morning sun, as high as it would be that day, beamed down through the stained glass body of St Michael—the archangel's foot securing the body of the serpent as he angled his spear toward its head. Both men left the church to the recessional melody of shrieks and screams from the occupant of the confession box. "Won't it burn the box?" Lacey asked. Muldoon shook his head.

"No. His type are quite self-contained, which is kind of them. The housekeeper will probably sweep it up thinking someone was smoking in there."

They descended the snow-dusted steps of St Michael's church where Andrew Gill was waiting for them.

"Is that the last one, then?" he asked with a sneer.

"I think so," Muldoon said, stopping to admire the sunbeams penetrating through the thick cloud. "All roads led to Father Brown. It stops with him."

Gill huffed. "What a strange world we live in. Vampires?"

"Yes. The very same. Uncannily like the kind you find in the penny dreadfuls."

"I used to love those when I was younger!" Lacey said, pulling his gloves back on.

"Aye, me too," Gill agreed. "End of an era now though. We've had our fill of vampires," he said, adjusting his collar. "Anyway, where the hell have you been?" He angled his interrogative eyes at the inspector.

"I told you," Muldoon began, "I took some time off."

"Will you be pisssing off for Easter too just in time for Father Brown's inevitable resurrection as well?"

Lacey quickly turned his head in surprise. "That happens?" he asked.

Muldoon shook his head. "No, it doesn't. And yes Gill, I might."

Gill regarded him for a moment. "Did you consider my offer, then?"

"I'm still thinking about it."

Gill grunted and turned his face away for a moment. "How was Christmas then?" he asked the inspector.

Muldoon, fondly remembering the holiday that had just passed, smiled and said, "not bad. Yours?"

"It was fine. If anyone asks me to play Charades one more time though, I'm packing my bags."

Muldoon chuckled. "I'm glad to be back."

"Well..." Gill looked about the deserted streets as the snow began to float down in feather-like flakes. "Pub? Seen as we missed New Year celebrations?"

As they began to exit the churchyard, Muldoon rubbed something with his forefinger and thumb in his pocket: a soft lock of mousy brown hair. "Yes," he said in response to Gill. "Let's hope it's a good one."

About the author

Hanna lives in her home city of Liverpool with her husband and three kids. She loves dogs, books, running, gaming and can't resist a ghost story. She studied English Literature BA and went on to complete a Literature MA at Liverpool Hope University before teaching English for several years. The Spider is her second novel. You can catch up with Hanna and see what she's working on at hannadelaneyauthor .com

Newsletter

Acknowledgements

WRITING A NOVEL IS no mean feat, and it can be a solitary existence when you're writing one. Firstly, my husband, who supported every idea, every draft and every moment that I needed to spend writing—thank you. I appreciated every proofreading session, every comment, and every critique. I would also like to thank my Substack subscribers and the wider fiction community of Substack. You are some of the most wonderful, encouraging people to be around. Thank you to Author Michele Bardsley for taking a new novelist under your wing and for helping me see the road ahead. Thank you to Michael and Lesley Gough, Alexandra Gilligan-Cook, Christina Murray, Autumn Thomson, Richard Ritenbaugh, Sergej Klementinovski and Sue Burch for your support throughout this project. I'd like to say a huge thank you to my ARC team, who are wonderful! Thank you to my best friend, Suzanne, who once said, "there are worse books out there, do you know what I mean?"— you're an absolute hero and I think about this every time I write. Thank you to Lee Robinson who made sure that I had an author website in order to look 'the real deal'.

Thank you to everyone who pre-ordered, shared and spread the word. I am eternally grateful. Here's to more books!

www.ingramcontent.com/pod-product-compliance
Ingram Content Group UK Ltd.
Pitfield, Milton Keynes, MK11 3LW, UK
UKHW041433180225
4643UKWH00028B/210